The Last Conception

by

Gabriel Constans

Published by
Melange Books, LLC
White Bear Lake, MN 55110
www.melange-books.com

The Last Conception ~ Copyright © 2014 by Gabriel Constans

ISBN: 978-1-61235-876-5

Names, characters, and incidents depicted in this book are products of the author's imagination or are used fictitiously. Any resemblance to actual events, locales, organizations, or persons, living or dead, is entirely coincidental and beyond the intent of the author or the publisher. No part of this book may be reproduced or transmitted in any form or by any means, electronic or mechanical, including photocopying, recording, or by any information storage and retrieval system, without permission in writing from the publisher.
Published in the United States of America.

Cover Art by Stephanie Flint

To love, in all its manifestations.

What reviewers are saying about The Last Conception

"Often, when tradition and technology meet they collide without forgiveness. Gabriel Constans manages to bring these opposites together with an open heart and the result is a story of compassion, love and the gifts that a generous partnership can provide."
    Syd Parker, best-selling author of *Secrets of the Heart, Love's Abiding Spirit* and I*mmediate Possession.*

"The Last Conception is a delightful read! It depicts a family muddling its way through a mire of personal, cultural, and generational differences, and reminds us all to slow down and remember—what else—love. Besides, what good are agendas when the dance of life is out of our control?"
    Joan Tewkesbury, award-winning filmmaker, screenwriter and novelist.

The Last Conception is a delightful read! It depicts a family muddling its way through a mire of personal, cultural, and generational differences, and reminds us all to slow down and remember—what else—love. Besides, what good are agendas when the dance of life is out of our control?
    Clifford Henderson, author of acclaimed *Spanking New* and *Mae's Request.*

"'The Last Conception' is a bhakti-fest of love and loss, hope and courage that comes in unexpected packages. Take a peek into the lives of an Indian-American family faced with an unusual demand of their medical professional unmarried daughter whose job and personal life intersect in unanticipated ways. Although happy endings are never guaranteed, it seems that one is in the offing for this savory literary masala.
    Edie Weinstein, author of *The Bliss Mistress Guide To Transforming the Ordinary Into the Extraordinary.*

The Last Conception is an engaging and unexpected tale of a young American woman whose choices about partnership and parenting have significant implications for her East Indian parents. According to them, it is Savarna's destiny to have a child, to continue the lineage of an ancient spiritual teacher. The novella is well written and fast-paced and evokes important inquires into spirituality and the true meaning of birth.

    Donna Baier Stein—author of the novel *Fortune* and award-winning short stories, including *The Yogi and the Peacock, El Nino, The Jewel Box, Coming Clean* and *Lambada*.

In The Last Conception, Gabriel Constans reaches into everyone's heart and mind. He explores the essence of religion, not as something prescribed, but as a suggestion of loving connectedness beyond time.

    Arny Mindell, author of *The Dreammaker's Apprentice* **and** *The Shaman's Body*.

The Last Conception is a compelling read. The mystery at the heart of this tale about the complicatons of conception lures the reader to examine the deeper issues facing the characters: telling the truth about one's needs and desires, the urge to have children, the pressures of family ancestry, and the power of love. Suspenseful and sweet, there's always an unexpected twist, all the way to the end.

    Marcy Alancraig—author of *A Woman of Heart*, accepted by the National Jewish Book Awards and Lambada Awards for a debut novel.

Chapter One

Savarna tried another yoga pose. "Damn," she said, losing her balance, just as the phone rang. She picked up her cell and answered.

"Hi, Sis. What's up?"

Savarna's sister, Chitra, had married Mike Nolan, an architect. Savarna loved him like the brother she'd never had. He was easy to get along with and always up for a joke or two, even if the joke was on him. Chitra and Mike were the same age. Their parents, Mira and Davidia Sikand, had been hesitant at first, since Mike had been raised Lutheran and wasn't, as they said, "from quite the right background." Her parents quickly came around when, after being married only six months, Chitra had been diagnosed with metastatic cancer. They saw their son-in-law lovingly and devoutly stay with their daughter through the horrendous but successful surgery, chemotherapy, and radiation. If it hadn't been for Mike's determination, energy, and positive attitude, they were not sure Chitra would have fared as well as she did. "Savarna, could you stop and pick up some drinks for Mom's party? It's the only thing I forgot."

"No problem. I'll get some juice and chai. You know how much she loves her chai."

They both grinned, certain the other was doing the same. Their mother could drink a gallon of chai and keep guzzling if more was offered. Then she would always complain that she had to go to the bathroom so often. It was a lifelong obsession that her children made fun of at every opportunity. When they were younger, some of their friends accidentally called their mother Mrs. Chai, having heard the girls calling her that themselves when she wasn't present.

"Well?" Chitra questioned.

"Well, what?" Savarna replied.

"Are you going to tell them?"

"Maybe. Don't make it a big deal, OK?"

"But it is a big deal. I think Mom knows anyway. You know how she likes to live in her dream world."

"Don't we all?"

"Starts at seven, so don't be late."

"Why would I be late?"

"Just drive for once, OK. You don't have to ride your bike everywhere, and don't start in on all that environmental stuff with me. I already get it and you know it."

Savarna laughed. "I guess I could use the car and show up on time."

"Well hello! Why get a car if you're never going to use it anyway?"

"I'll be there at seven sharp."

"With the drinks."

"With the drinks."

"And Mom's present."

"Present?" Savarna paused. "I thought she said she didn't want any presents, only donations to that religious group she and Dad belong to.

"She doesn't, but I thought we could chip in and buy the airfare for their yearly pilgrimage."

"They've managed to do that on their own ever since we were born."

"Yes, but it hasn't been easy, and it's not like you and I are poor. Don't you think it would be a nice gesture and show of support, even though we know it's all hogwash?"

"Point taken. How much were you thinking?"

"A thousand. If we each pitch in that amount, it will almost cover them both for a round trip."

"You've got it."

"See you later."

"Ciao."

* * * *

"Happy fifty-eighth, Mom!" Savarna exclaimed, as her mother and father came out of the kitchen. They hurried to their daughter and gave her a big hug and lots of kisses.

"Hold on here," Savarna said, stepping back for a moment. "It's your birthday, not mine." Her parents grinned and hugged her some more.

"Let me put these drinks in the kitchen, before I drop them."

"You didn't bring any chai, did you?" her mother asked.

"Of course not," Savarna replied. "Why on earth would we? Everyone knows you hate the stuff."

"Really?"

"Of course I brought some, and it's freshly made."

"Hello!" Chitra yelled, as she and Mike came in the front door. They put down their pots and bowls and greeted her mother and father.

"Is Savarna here already? I can't believe she got here before us."

"You saw her car in the driveway," Mike said, with a few laugh lines rising next to his blue eyes.

"I know, but it's hard to believe she actually drove it."

"Is it that electric one she's been talking about?" asked Savarna's father.

"Sure is," Mike said.

"You want to take a look?"

"Indeed."

As Mike and Davidia went outside to evaluate the car, Chitra and her mother joined Savarna in the kitchen.

"I'll put the naan in the oven while you heat up the chai," Chitra told her sister.

"Here," Mira said, grabbing the pot out of Savarna's hands. "Let me do that."

"No way," Savarna said, reclaiming the pot and placing it on the burner. "It's your birthday, let us do it for a change."

The girls playfully tried to push their mother out of the kitchen. She protested and tickled them. They tickled her back until all three women were giggling like young schoolgirls.

"Stop! Stop!" Chitra squealed in between rolling rounds of laughter. "You're going to make me pee my pants."

"You're wearing a dress," Savarna laughed, brushing her hand over her sister's short jet-black hair. "How can you pee your pants?" She and her mother ganged up on Chitra and tickled her again.

Chitra slid to the floor. "If I had on pants, they'd be soaked."

Savarna and her mother stopped tickling Chitra and helped her up off the floor.

"If anybody is going to pee their pants, it's going to be Mom," Savarna said, "*after* she drinks all that chai!"

Their mother slapped Savarna's shoulder and said, with mock surprise, "How could you ever say such a thing?"

Once they regained a modicum of composure, their mother said, "I can see that you and Mike are happy. Your union has been such a blessing for all of us."

"Absolutely. You picked a good one, Sis," Saverna replied.

"Which reminds me," their mother interjected. "There's something we should talk about."

"OK," Savarna replied and glanced at her sister, who smiled back. "There's something I want to talk about with you too."

"I'll leave you two at it," Chitra said. "I'm going to look at your latest technological marvel. Where are the keys?"

"In the side pocket of my purse. Help yourself."

"I'll bet those guys didn't even think of getting the keys so they could turn the damn thing on."

As Chitra left to join her husband and father gawking at the vehicle outside, Mira took Savarna's hand and led her to the living room couch. The couch was old but in perfect condition. They'd picked it out twenty years ago, when they decided to "modernize" their home furnishings.

"So."

"So."

"I've found the perfect man for you. He's bright, handsome, well off, and wants to marry an Indian girl like you, and before you say 'No,' he's also a scientist. He works at the Berkeley Labs with energy alternatives, or something like that. You both have a lot in common. He's different from anyone else I've ever told you about."

Savarna sighed deeply and calmed herself before she replied. "Mom, first off, I'm not an 'Indian' girl, I'm as American as they come."

"You know what I—"

The Last Conception

"Second, I don't care if he's the smartest man in the world or looks like a movie star."

"But—"

"Thirdly, I'll bet my ever-loving mother that you've never even met this fellow and only heard about him from your matchmaker friend, Mrs. Padhamasa, right?"

"Well," her mother said, shaking her head side to side in defeat.

"Mom, you and Dad have been trying to get me married off since I was sixteen. If it hasn't worked after all these years, why do you think it will now?"

"It's not a matter of 'thinking' or 'wishing.' It is an urgent and necessary step which we will never stop pursuing until you are wed and have children."

"Mom—" Savarna hung her head— "believe me. It will never happen."

"Why not? I know you're older, but you're still pretty. Any man worth his salt would want you for his wife."

"You don't understand."

"I'm not dumb. Is there something I should know?"

"Mom…"

The front door burst open. "I'll be," exclaimed Mr. Sikand. "That is really something."

"It's amazing!" Mike piped in. "We should get one of those."

"I'm with you, dear," Chitra replied. "I smell something. Did you check the naan Savarna?"

"Oh no." She bolted towards the kitchen.

"The one thing I ask you to do and you forget all about it," Chitra said, as she followed her sister towards the burning bread.

Davidia looked at Mira.

"No," Mira said, standing. She adjusted her orange-yellow sari over her shoulder and pushed back her braided gray hair. "She wouldn't even look at the picture."

"We've got to do something," Davidia said, embracing his wife of forty years. "We might have to take drastic action."

"Like what, kidnap her and marry her against her will?"

"Don't talk crazy," he said. He brushed his hand over his receding

5

hairline.

"If it only concerned us—" Mira's face contorted— "it would be a different matter."

"I know. I know," he said, taking Mira's hand and leading her toward the kitchen. "Come on, birthday girl. Today's your day. We'll figure out how to get a grandchild born soon enough."

Chapter Two

Savarna was the first to arrive at five that morning. She placed her bicycle in the storage room, washed-up, and put on her scrubs. She checked all of the incubators, work surfaces, and electronic readouts, to make sure everything was operating as close to body temperature as possible. The machines were on twenty-four seven and alarmed. After all, she and her colleagues literally held the possibility of new life in their hands day after day. If anything goes out of whack, emergency calls are automatically made until someone responds. They have backup systems for backup systems. So far, in her eight years of working at Conception Sciences, the alarm had gone off only once, and that turned out to be a faulty reading.

"Hey, Embryo Mama, how are our babies doing?"

Savarna had just started looking at the results from the previous day when her work partner, Johnny Cranston, walked in. She'd known Johnny for five years and trusted him completely. If she were ever in the position of their patients, she'd want Johnny to be her embryologist. He was very tech-savvy and gave a damn. Personally, he'd been through the ringer: he was divorced and had his adored teenage daughter living with him part-time. He'd recently moved to a nice neighborhood just twenty minutes from work. Johnny was handsome, and he knew it, but he never let his guard down, especially in front of beautiful women. He considered Savarna to fall in the category of beautiful, but she was an exception to his well-practiced defenses.

"Good morning, Sperm Daddy," she replied.

"Where we at, darling? Everything cooking at the right temp?"

"I was just checking yesterday's records and laying out our schedule. Will you take a look and sign off?"

"It would be my pleasure."

Savarna always noticed the contrasts between them when they stood side by side. He had big hands with long fingers. She was brown, like a lightly baked brownie, and he was as black as dark chocolate. He stood a foot taller, had broad shoulders, a muscular chest and shaved head. She had long jet-black hair braided and tied up in a knot for work, a distinguished nose, and hips that seemed to trump everything else from the waist down.

"Looks like we've got a lot of D1 and D3s to switch out today," Johnny said, as he signed the checklist.

"Yes, and two D5s. I really hope Mrs. Schneider's takes this time and her Inner Cell Mass doesn't get screwed up like her last two attempts. She was so devastated."

"You got that right. Nothing we could do though. Hear what I'm saying?"

"Yeah, yeah. I know the mantra. Don't beat ourselves up for what's out of our control."

"Well, well. You actually remember your own advice."

They both chuckled underneath their masks.

Everything in the laboratory had to be done perfectly and on schedule. Mistakes were not allowed, though they were inevitable.

Day zero, which they referred to as D0, was egg retrieval day. That was when they retrieved eggs from the woman and sperm from the man and put them together in a dish. On Day One, which they called D1, they checked to see how many of the eggs were fertilized. They looked through the microscope to see if there were two pronuclei inside. If they couldn't see any or what they saw consisted of only one or three pronuclei, that meant it was a wash and they couldn't be used.

Day Two was when the embryos started to divide. A healthy embryo consisted of two to four cells. That was when Savarna and Johnny would start to grade or evaluate the embryos on a scale of one to five, with one being perfect and five being poor. It took about one minute to look at fifteen embryos. They had to do it quickly, so they were not outside of the incubator for long, otherwise they could die.

The Last Conception

Day Three should have shown six to eight cells per embryo. If some of these were healthy, they could transfer them on the same day or put them into an extended culture for a Day Five transfer.

On Day Five embryos would have grown much bigger and gone from six to eight cells to fifty to one hundred cells. This was the day when transfer usually took place. One to two embryos were transferred to the patient's uterus. Any extras were frozen or cultured to Day Six.

On Day Six, anything that is left was either frozen or discarded.

"You can have the honor of icing any leftovers today," Savarna told Johnny.

"Thank you, great ice queen. It will be an honor to preserve someone who may one day be our next Albert Einstein or Maya Angelou."

"Or Charlie Manson or Hitler," she said, half-joking.

"Not possible. These children are too wanted and adored to turn out like that."

Freezing embryos was no minor task, though it may appear to be a simple procedure. When a healthy and viable embryo was frozen, it was placed into a computer-driven freezer in liquid nitrogen and slowly brought down to minus thirty-five degrees centigrade. When cells were frozen they were made up mostly of water and had to be dehydrated before freezing or ice cycles could destroy them. They were passed through solutions that by osmosis moved in and out of a fluid buffer. Freezing took about an hour and a half. When they were thawed, it was important to get rid of the ice crystals right away, so they are pulled out, held in the air for thirty counts, and put in a thirty-degree water bath for forty-five seconds until they were thawed. They were then placed in solutions that reversed the process and put water back in. Within forty minutes of being de-thawed, an embryo could be transferred. Some patients successfully used an embryo that had been frozen for over ten years.

* * * *

Savarna and Johnny sent out the morning report to all the physicians and case managers by 7:30, so they would know which patients to call to come in for their procedures or which ones needed to change their medications. Then they started working on egg retrievals, sperm analysis, and triple-verification with each, to make sure they had the correct specimen for each individual. Retrievals started around 8:00 a.m. and continued every forty-five minutes, while transfers generally began at 10:00 and took place every thirty minutes. By noon, they were inseminating the eggs. Somewhere in the controlled chaos, they tried to make their way to the bathroom and catch a bite to eat. At 1:00 they made a break for the small lunchroom squeezed into the back corner of the two-story medical building.

Johnny took a big bite of his sandwich, gulped down some soda and stared at Savarna.

"What?" she asked, looking up from her salad bowl.

"Come on. I'm about to burst. Did you tell them?"

Savarna smiled, took a drink from her homemade chocolate smoothie, and sheepishly looked down at her Greek salad.

"You've got to be kidding."

She shook her head. "My Mom was—"

"This is crazy…after all these years. They're adults. They'll understand."

"Let me explain."

"What's there to explain? You chickened out again."

"No, I didn't. We were interrupted. My mother was trying to get me married off for the umpteenth time and just as I was about to tell her why I would never marry a man, the rest of the family burst in. There wasn't any good time after that. It was her birthday after all, and I didn't want to ruin it."

"Ruin it?"

"You don't understand."

"Try me."

"In Indian culture marriage is the biggest and most important celebration there is."

"And you don't think that's true for other cultures?"

"Well, yes, of course," she replied, taking a deep breath and looking him straight in the eyes. "But in India it can actually be a matter of life and death. Women are still defined by whom, when, and if they marry. I don't care if this is California and my parents have lived here for decades. I don't think they even realize how deep this tradition is ingrained in their psyches."

"So, it's fair to keep them in the dark and keep hoping?"

"Of course not, but I'm not always as strong or as confident with my family as I am with you. I don't want to hurt them."

"I think you're hurting them more, let alone yourself, by not standing up and letting yourself be counted. They just want you to be happy, and they see marriage as the means to attain that happiness. We both know it's not always what it's cracked up to be, but I don't see anything wrong with them hoping it's the answer for their spinster daughter whose childbearing clock is ticking."

"Spinster, my ass."

"Tell them I'll take you off their hands, but only for a good dowry."

Savarna raised her glass, as if to throw it in Johnny's face. He backed up his chair in mock surprise. Savarna's phone rang. She put down her cup, laughing, and took the call.

"Hi, Magdalena. What's up?"

Johnny winked.

"Tonight? It's only Monday."

Savarna closed her eyes for a moment as she listened.

"Which club?"

She nodded. "OK. OK. Pick me up at nine." She clicked her phone shut and put it on the table while Johnny went to the sink to put away his plate.

"She's a wild woman," he said upon returning to the table.

"It's fun. Nothing serious."

"Yeah, I know about fun, but is that all you want?"

Her phone rang again.

"Hey, Charley. How ya doing?"

Johnny rolled his eyes.

"This weekend? I don't know, I'm usually pretty wiped out by then."

She turned away slightly in her chair, as if to keep the conversation private.

"In that case, let's do it. I'll call you later. Take care."

"Wish I had that many women calling me up," Johnny wisecracked, as they stood and both prepared to re-gown and get back to work. "Where to this weekend?"

"Charley got a great deal on a bed and breakfast place in the redwoods over in Santa Cruz. She says it's just what I need for some rest and relaxation."

"So, you really prefer men after all."

"You know Charley is—"

"I know, I know. Just goofing. You know my offer is always good. If you ever want to get turned around, I'll show you what a real man is like."

"Yeah." They both laughed. "You and a thousand other men."

"Hey, did you hear what one egg said to another when they saw millions of sperm on the horizon?"

"Only a zillion times," she said. They made their way down the hall and entered the pressurized lab. "But if it floats your boat, go ahead and give me the punch line. I'll act like I've never heard it before."

"Now you've ruined it," he said.

The automatic door opened and she went ahead. A cartoon they had taped on the door had two eggs and millions of sperm surrounding them. The caption next to the first egg read, "This doesn't look good, I think the odds are against us." The other egg said, "Looks good to me. It's just what the doctor ordered."

Chapter Three

Dance Your Ass Off was unusually crowded for a Monday night in San Francisco. The music and customers were just as loud as any other time of the week, and Magdalena and Savarna were sweating like long-haired Alaskan Huskies that had been dropped off on the pavement of Miami in the middle of a sweltering summer.

"Eeehaa!" Magdalena screamed to the pounding beat as her long black hair flew from side to side, covering her dripping face.

Savarna tried to keep up but was always one step behind. She could feel Magdalena's breath on her skin as she moved closer and their hips swayed side to side. Magdalena ran her hand up Savarna's back and planted her lips in the middle of her neck.

"Lena! Lena!" someone yelled.

Magdalena gave a parting lick and turned to see who had intruded into their moment.

"Christy!"

Christy and Magdalena embraced as if their lives depended on it. Then Magdalena grabbed Christy's hand and led her across the floor to Savarna.

"Christy, this is my gorgeous girl, Savarna."

"Wow, you aren't kidding. She is beautiful."

Savarna pointed at herself. "Me?"

"Beautiful and hot as a candlestick," Magdalena added. "Savarna, this is Christy."

Savarna offered her hand, but Christy moved in and gave her a bear hug, then stepped back, but not very far back. "Yes, before you ask," Christy said, "we were an item, but that was a long time ago." Christy grinned.

"Yeah, it's been at least a month or two," Magdalena laughed.

Savarna's forced smile vanished.

"Just kidding," said Magdalena. "I haven't seen this fine thing for almost two years."

"Come on," Christy said. "Come meet my sweetheart. We've got a place over there in the corner. You can almost hear what you're saying."

The music stopped momentarily. They made their way to the booth, where it looked like a fashion-model showroom mannequin had been stuffed into the seat. The music started up again at full volume, with "Fearless Love" by Melissa Etheridge snaking its way through everyone's eardrums. The mannequin's head turned and stared right through them.

"I'd like you to meet Pam," Christy said. She slid in next to the now moving mannequin and gave her a killer hug and kiss.

"It's a pleasure, I'm sure." Pam smiled.

"The pleasure is ours," Magdalena replied. She and Savarna slid into the opposite side.

"No, it's mine," Christy said, raising her eyebrows, turning Pam's head and giving her such a long, passionate kiss that it seemed as if she was going to devour her right then and there.

When they came up for air and Pam straightened up and touched her face to make sure everything was in place, Magdalena said, "You haven't changed."

"No, I haven't, thank God," Christy said. "But I get the feeling you've gone a little domestic on me." She nodded towards Savarna. "Does she know what you're like? I mean really know?"

Magdalena gave Savarna a kiss on the cheek. "Of course she knows. Don't you, baby?" Savarna nodded. "She's not as prim and proper as she looks. When she lets loose, she can be a wildcat, just like you." Christy cocked her head sideways and grinned. "OK, not like you. Nobody is just like you, but we've got a good thing going."

"Hey, don't look at me," Christy said. "You don't have to say anything. I know a good thing when I see it." She looked at Savarna, then at Pam. "I know it's hard to believe, but Pam teaches third grade in Mountain View."

"I guess you've always had a thing for teachers," Magdalena said.

"Lena teaches history of the Americas at Santa Clara Catholic University," Christy explained to Pam. "You aren't still attending Mass, are you?"

Savarna stiffened and stared at Magdalena.

"Well, yes, I am. What's it to you?"

"Nothing." Christy laughed. "Nothing at all. It just never made sense to me, that's all. I mean… you are who you are."

"*You* go to Mass?" Savarna exclaimed.

"What I believe and what I do don't always go hand in hand. You know what I'm saying?" Magdalena leaned towards Savarna and kissed her, then turned back to Christy. "And you, you still defending the poor helpless insurance companies?"

"Not as much. I'm working part-time as a court-appointed lawyer. The money sucks, but it's good for my conscience."

"What about you?" Pam nodded at Savarna. "What are you into?"

"You mean, besides me?" Magdalena grinned.

"I work with IVF."

"IV what?" Pam asked.

"It's probably the International Venus Fellowship," Christy exclaimed.

"In Vitro Fertilization," Savarna said. "I'm an embryologist."

"You help people have babies?" Pam said.

"Yes."

"That always seemed weird to me." Christy shook her head. "Why on earth would anybody put themselves through that? If it was meant to be, so be it. If not, let it be."

Savarna felt Magdalena's fingertips tighten under the table, as they rested just above her knee.

"Having a baby is arguably the strongest desire we have. It's in our DNA. I doubt we'd have much of a human race without it," Savarna said, as calmly as she could muster.

"Yeah, but to do it artificially and have to mess around with all that sperm and guck, yuck," Christy said.

"It's really more sterile than an operating room," Savarna said. "And there's nothing artificial about it. We just help increase the odds of conception and create the best environment possible for the baby to grow. The mother is the one who does all the work."

"What's so complicated?" Christy said. "You just take a turkey baster, shoot it up in there, and wait for nine months."

Savarna laughed, as Magdalena's hand slowly slid higher up her leg. "I wish it were that easy. Do you have any idea what a woman goes through to have this work?"

Christy shook her head.

"First, she has to be inseminated at just the right time of the month. Then, she has to start taking meds that stimulate her ovaries. We have to suppress the natural hormone production in order to control the cycle. Instead of getting just one dominant egg, she is getting them coming all at once."

"What was that?" Christy almost shouted, as they all leaned forward to hear over the music.

"I said," Savarna continued with a raised voice, "the average stimulation is about ten to twelve days of injectable hormones. It's like a little pen they stick in their stomach. After implantation the real fun begins, when they get to take a hormone shot in their butt for about eight weeks. Some women's bottoms get so sore, it's difficult for them to sit down comfortably."

Magdalena's hand grabbed Savarna's thigh and kept creeping up between her legs.

"OK, OK, but—" Christy was cut off, as Savarna continued.

"The good news is that you get a lot of eggs, but the bad news is that you can't always control the environment. If you put her on hormones and she only has three or four follicles, you can't just start giving her more hormones to get more. And if somebody has a huge response, that can cause over-stimulation with medical consequences. It's really a fine-tuned process… a balancing act that needs to be tailor-made to each individual patient." Magdalena's hand had just reached her crotch. Savarna grabbed it and pushed it away. "Sometimes patients go through all this time, expense, discomfort, and expectation, and their ovaries don't do anything. Others have everything working just fine, but the endometria's lining won't hold the embryo and grow at the same rate. It can be heartbreaking."

"Why don't they just adopt?" Pam asked quietly.

"Why don't you like sex with men?" Savarna challenged.

"I just wasn't made that way."

"Well, there you go. We're each different, right? We all have different desires, needs, and biology. If you—"

"Hear that?" Magdalena asked, grabbing Savarna by the arm and trying to pull her up. "It's an old Donna Summer classic. Let's dance."

"No, I've heard this crap for so long. I'm sick of all the judgments."

"Come on, darling, calm down. They're just asking."

"And I'm just answering. Go ahead and dance. I'm not stopping you."

"Well, I'm not going to pass this one up," Christy replied. She jumped up, grabbed Magdalena's hand and took her to the floor that was once again getting jam-packed.

"Aren't there thousands of kids that need homes already?" Pam insisted, leaning in closer to hear.

"Yes and a lot of people are adopting them. Some adoptive parents knew that is what they wanted to do. Others tried everything in the book to have a biological child, and it never worked out. And quite a few go through successful IVF, have a healthy birth child AND adopt another child later on."

"It seems so complicated and time-consuming. I don't know why anybody would want to raise children. They are such a hassle. I'm exhausted after being with them six hours a day and they aren't even mine."

"You've never thought of having a child? Never wondered what it feels like to be pregnant, hold a baby you created in your arms and have it suckle your breast for nourishment and life?"

Pam lowered her eyes and sat back. "There was a time, but it seems so long ago." She looked up to see if Savarna was still listening. "I'd just graduated from high school and was still a little confused. My parents wanted me to go to college and get married. I went out with a few men to see what it was like and, like an idiot, got pregnant." She looked towards the wall then gazed out the open door. "He said I should get an abortion, but against all reason I decided to keep it." She paused, as a tear slid along the side of her nose. "Two months later I had a miscarriage. I thought I'd be relieved, but…" More tears flowed. "I had no idea how attached I had become to that baby. Everyone kept saying to just get over it. That I could get pregnant anytime I wanted to."

"That's such a big loss. I'm sorry."

"Yeah, well…" Pam sniffled, "I promised myself I'd never go through that again, and when I figured out who I was I knew it wouldn't be hard to keep that promise."

Christy and Magdalena both returned and collapsed in the booth. "She still has promise," Christy said, catching her breath.

"You're not bad yourself for such an old lady," Magdalena said and then kissed Savarna. "Let's hit the road and head on home," she said.

"I've got a feeling you're hitting more than the road tonight," Christy said with a grin.

Savarna reached over the table, took Pam's hand in hers and whispered, "Give me a call sometime. Here's my card." She reached in her pocket and handed Pam her number.

"What's going on here?" Christy asked. "We're gone two minutes and you two are hooking up."

"We were just talking about something," Savarna said as she rose from the table.

"Yeah, that's what everyone says," Christy said.

Pam took Christy's hand and led her towards the bar. "Let's get a drink. I'll tell you what it's about."

"OK, whatever you say."

"Good to see you, Christy," Magdalena said, as parting hugs ensued.

"Great to see you too, Lena," Christy replied. "Nice to reconnect."

Magdalena dropped off Savarna, then got out of the car to follow her inside. Savarna turned and put her hand on Magdalena's chest.

"Not tonight. I've got to get up early."

"Come on, babe, just a while. I'm so hot for you I'm about to boil over."

"Well," Savarna said with a grin. "I guess you'll just have to take the pot off the stove and let off a little steam all by yourself." She smiled and kissed Magdalena on the lips.

"What's going on? I could see that look of yours when we were dancing. I'm not blind."

"You've got excellent eyesight. I really wanted you then, but right now—"

"Did I do something wrong?"

Savarna caressed Magdalena's face. "Not a thing. You are wonderful and I had a great time, but talking with Pam and Christy about babies got me thinking."

"About what?"

"I don't know. Things just changed. I get so pissed with all the judgments people have about other peoples' lives."

Magdalena took Savarna's hands in hers. "That was then, this is now. Let me help you forget all about it."

"You're sweet, but not tonight. I'll call you later."

"You sure?"

"Yes, I'm sure."

She watched Magdalena walk back to her car and waved as she drove away.

That is perhaps the only thing I'm sure about at all these days. I thought I knew who I was, but I don't have a goddamn clue. Is everything really determined by our biology and DNA, or do we have choices and dreams that are from our own creation?

Savarna went to bed but couldn't sleep. In less than four hours she'd be back at work, helping to bring a new life into the world.

Chapter Four

"Throw your suitcase in the trunk and come on board." Charlemagne Burnell, known to her close friends as Charley, shouted from the car window.

Savarna slid her overnight case in the rear and got in the passenger side of the small, comfortable blue sedan. Charley leaned across the console and kissed Savarna.

"I've been looking forward to this all week," Savarna said.

"Me too," Charley said. "The place sounds fantastic, and I will never get tired of walking among the ancients."

"Absolutely. It always reminds me how insignificant we really are." Savarna reached over and put her hand on Charley's hip. "Thanks for putting this together. I'm usually so ramped up and busy all week, I never think about taking a break or having some down time."

"I know you don't. That's why I'm here."

Savarna laughed. She knew Charley was always looking out for her, and that was partly what made her uncomfortable. Sometimes Charley thought about her too often and didn't give herself enough attention.

As if reading her mind, Charley added, "Hey, it's not like there's nothing in this for me. Two nights in the redwoods with nothing to do but enjoy the company of my love and lounge in the silence."

That was the kicker. Savarna knew how deeply Charley loved her, and she wasn't yet sure if she felt the same, at least not in the same way. She was definitely attracted to Charley, felt at home when they were together and knew she could tell her anything, but… she knew Charley wanted more. Charley wanted the whole package and had told her so.

The Last Conception

She wasn't sure if she was ready for that or ever would be.

A half hour later, as they drove slowly through a light rain in the Santa Cruz Mountains on Highway 17, Charley switched on the radio.

"And this is the word of God," a vibrating voice exclaimed through the speakers.

"Oh no!" Charley exclaimed. "Switch it quick. I don't want to ruin the weekend listening to that garbage."

"Wait," Savarna said, stopping Charley's hand midway to the controls. "Give them a minute. I'm curious. I wonder what he's peddling."

Charley gave Savarna a puzzled look but let it be and put her hand back on the steering wheel.

"You shall love your neighbor as yourself," the man continued. "That is the Lord's second greatest commandment, to love one another."

"The problem with that is that most folks who believe it forget about the 'love yourself' part," Charley said. "They never feel that good about themselves or think they're enough, so they project their sense of inadequacy and judgment on to others. They're the first ones to tell you and me what we should believe and how we should live."

"Do I note a little judgment in your tone, young lady?" Savarna said with a deep voice.

"Ah, you got me." Charley grinned. "You know it's all hypocritical."

"All? I don't know if it's ALL hypocritical, but I know what you mean."

"God so loved the world that he gave his only Son," the radio preacher continued.

"That's enough," Charley said, turning off the radio. "I thought we were all God's children. How could 'He' give his only Son, if we're all made in 'His' image?"

"Sometimes you sound just like a lawyer; dissecting every word."

"Are you insinuating that I've become my mother?"

"No." Savarna laughed. "You don't come close to her French accent or profession, but you let other people's beliefs get you all riled up. This is just some guy spouting off on the radio like thousands of others."

"Yeah, I know… but it's not just words. It's this kind of dogma that can lead people to do stupid things and hurt others in the name of their God. Aren't your parents involved in some kind of religious cult or something themselves?"

"It's not a cult. It's some group they meet up with every year in India. They've never told me much about it, but I know they never try to get anyone else to join. They pray and meditate a lot but always kept me out of the loop. I've never been interested anyway, but I don't mind listening to other people's opinions every now and then and getting a lay of the land."

"Well," Charley said, "I had enough 'laying of the land' from friends and relatives to cover the entire state. You know my parents have always been cool about my love life, but you couldn't say that for the rest of the family. And some of my so-called friends dropped me like I was toxic when they found out. There was one girl in high school who told me I was living the life of the devil and needed to repent and go straight. I told her to go to hell."

"At least your parents know and totally love you," Savarna said. "Even after they separated."

"Yes, they do, and someone else's parents I know would probably do the same."

"Don't get started."

"How long have we been seeing each other? Two years?"

"About that, yeah."

"How often during the time we've been together have I told you to talk to your parents?"

Savarna thought for a moment. "Two, maybe three times."

"You're the one pressuring yourself to say something. My God, how couldn't you be thinking about it when they're trying to marry you off left and right?" Charley paused and cleared her throat. "You know I know how hard it is, but you also know how freeing it will be to stop hiding and keeping things under the rug."

"You mean in the closet."

"In the closet, under the rug, behind closed doors, whatever."

Savarna looked out the window and saw a deer and its fawn leaping away from the road up a steep hill. She thought about how tough a deer's life must be with so many humans having invaded their territory with fences, houses, roads, cars and concrete cities. It was amazing how well they adapted and survived.

"You know I love you, whether you tell them or not," Charley added.

"I know."

"It's your choice. I'm just saying you should give them a chance."

"I know. I guess I'm still afraid of what they'll say or do."

"Maybe that's what real faith is all about."

"Maybe."

* * * *

They lay on their backs, exhausted from their last tidal wave of lovemaking, and looked up at the knotted-pine beamed ceiling of their cabin near Felton, a small mountain town twenty minutes from the coastal city of Santa Cruz.

"Wow," Charley sighed.

"Definitely wow," Savarna exclaimed. "Those beams are amazing!"

"I meant..."

"I know," Savarna giggled. She turned and laid her head on Charley's shoulder. "I was just kidding."

"You coyote you," Charley said. She ran her hand down Savarna's spine and started to tickle her rib cage. "Always a jokester."

"Hardly always," she replied. She moved on top of Charley and held down her hands.

"I give. You can have me."

"I just did," Savarna smiled, then kissed Charley's lips. She inhaled the familiar scent. "You taste like me."

"I hope so, considering where I've been."

"Was it good?"

"It was very good," Charley grinned, just before kissing Savarna again. "How'd I get so lucky?"

"It wasn't luck, my dear," Savarna replied and laid her head on Charley's chest. "It was choice, and I have good taste."

The rose-patterned gauze curtains fluttered as a slight breeze made its way through the open window. Small animal feet could be heard making their way through the ferns outside: a raccoon looking for dinner.

Then Savarna's attention was drawn back to Charley. She noticed her breath was shallower and her chest had tightened.

"What is it?"

"What?"

"What are you thinking?"

"Nothing."

"You're the worst liar I've ever known. Out with it."

Savarna turned on her side, propping her head up on her hand. "You're still seeing Magdalena aren't you?"

"Yeah. That's no secret. Is there a problem with that?"

"It's no problem for me, but I think it may be for you."

Savarna sat up and pulled the sheet around her to keep warm. "What are you implying?"

"It's not an implication, it's an observation." Charley said, as she lifted her petit frame and crossed her legs to sit facing Savarna. She took her pillow and placed it on her lap.

Savarna admired the blue eyes and short pixie-cut blond hair of her inquisitor in the dim light from the bedside lamp.

"I'm waiting."

"I think you already know what I'm going to say, but here it goes anyway." Charley put her hand lightly on Savarna's calf. "I'm in love with you and have been ever since we met, and I believe you feel the same." Savarna didn't reply. "I'm ready to settle down and even consider having kids." Savarna straightened her back and took a deep breath. "You don't think you're ready and keep acting out with Magdalena to convince yourself."

"You think I—"

"Let me finish." Charley took both of Savarna's hands in hers. "It seems like you're afraid of something, but I don't know exactly what it is. Maybe it's the idea of commitment or a sense that you'll lose your freedom." She kissed Savarna's long, soft fingers. "Or more likely, it's because you would then be forced to tell your parents, since you can't hide who you live with." Savarna pulled her hands away.

"I thought we already spoke about this on the way here, and you said you'd drop it."

"We did, but you asked me what I was thinking about and there it is.

The Last Conception

You don't like to talk about it or have me bring it up, but I can see it's eating you up night and day."

Savarna looked down at her hands, still wet from Charley's kiss. "You might be right. I don't think you understand what this could do to my family. It's not just about tradition and culture, it's literally taboo to talk about it, let alone to be it. They'd see it as throwing burning coals in their face, something I was doing to hurt them."

"Savarna, you're an intelligent and brave woman, but I think it's your fear of the unknown that's holding you back, and you're using all these reasons as excuses. They probably know more than you've ever given them credit for."

"Let's get some sleep," Savarna said. She lay down and pulled the blankets up around her shoulders.

"OK," Charley said, lying down. "Let's take it up with our old friends tomorrow morning. Those ancient redwoods are great listeners."

Charley fell fast asleep, but Savarna's mind couldn't stop babbling. It kept playing one scenario after another, and none of them had a happy ending.

* * * *

Savarna awoke at dawn. Even though it was a day off and the weekend, her internal clock was still set to rise and get moving. She lay as still as she could, not wanting to wake Charley, but after a few minutes she knew it would be impossible to go back to sleep. She got up as quietly as possible and slipped on her pants, thick denim shirt and walking boots, wishing she'd brought a warm jacket and gloves. They could have turned on the heating system, but they didn't like the artificial heat and had decided to live with the morning cold, which they both knew was inevitable under the canopy of the redwoods, which were always in collusion with the drippy fog and mist. As she put on her heavy woolen coat, she gazed back at Charley, who shifted ever so slightly. She had to admit she never got tired of seeing that lovely face and those luscious lips. She turned and opened the door without a peep, but the screen squeaked.

"Savarna?"

"Yeah, hon."

"Where you going?" Charley said. She stretched and smiled. Savarna went back to the edge of the bed and sat down.

"Just a short walk down to the river." Their cabin was on a hill just 500 feet from the San Lorenzo River, which wound its way through the San Lorenzo Valley in the Santa Cruz Mountains. "I didn't want to wake you. You looked so sweet and peaceful."

Charley wrapped her arms around Savarna and gave her a kiss. "I must have been dreaming about you."

"I hope it was me."

"There is nobody else."

"Well, you just go ahead and lounge." Savarna pulled the covers back up over Charley and tucked them in around her neck. "I won't be gone long. I'm going to have a talk with those tall friends of ours."

"Ah, the ancients. They always have the answer."

"I'm sure they do," Savarna said, as she made her way to the door. "But I don't always understand their language."

* * * *

Savarna slowly descended on the path down to the river. She walked carefully, to not lose her footing and not wanting to disturb the peace and quiet that pervaded the redwoods around her, whispering in their silent thousand-year-old tongue.

"You must have seen a lot of life pass this way," she said. "I'll bet you get pretty tired of hearing all the melodrama and crazy things people say and do." At that very moment a twig snapped under her boot, as if to say, "You've got that right." "Well, here's another one for you, though I'm sure this is nothing new." She slipped, caught hold of a branch and continued downward. "How do you know when you're with the right person? I mean, how do you really know?" A squirrel suddenly sounded the alarm of her approach. She followed the sound and watched the bushy-tailed gray rodent hop along a long branch and then scamper up the trunk.

"As I was saying." She continued walking. "There's got to be some sign, some data or information I could analyze and make a valid determination."

She got to the river and let herself be swept away with the sound of

The Last Conception

the rushing water. There was something about rivers that had always called her to their shores. Ever since she had read *Siddhartha* by Hesse as a teenager, she'd believed that rivers held some kind of truth or metaphor for everything in life, and those who felt likewise were part of a community of people that understood this reality. Now, here she was, alone, watching the water flow. She continued the conversation she'd been having with the redwoods. "Everything about her feels right, but settling down... kids... that's something else. Look at you. You never stop. You're always changing, on the go, adapting to the course you've been given." She reached down into the mud and found a flat stone, swung her arm sideways and watched the rock skip three times across the rippling waves of water. She pulled the back of her coat down over her bottom and sat on a wet log that had fallen by the water's edge.

"OK, you won't let me in on the secret, but I know that you know." She heard many sounds, but no answers. "What about this," she continued. "How do you tell someone you love something that you know they will not understand, but you have to tell them anyway?"

After a half hour of reflection and a seemingly one-sided conversation, Savarna walked up the hill, touching the bark of her ancient friends along the way. Before she opened the door to the cabin, she smelled eggs and toast.

She entered, took off her wet coat, and hung it on the back of a wooden chair.

"You should have slept in longer."

"I couldn't any more than you could," Charley said while she dished up breakfast and handed the plate to Savarna.

"Thanks," Savarna said. She put down her plate and poured them both a cup of the coffee Charley had brewed.

"Let's sit out front."

Savarna grabbed a blanket to wrap around them both, then they sat on the porch swing and placed the plates in their laps and their cups on the side rails. The old swing was pretty stationary because of the accumulation of rust in its springs.

"So, what did they say?" Charley asked after ten minutes of silence.

"They?"

Charley nodded toward the forest.

Savarna smiled shyly. "Nothing new really. They pretty much said I have to figure things out on my own and make my own choices. You know, their usual words of wisdom."

"And what, per se, where you asking?"

"The usual." She took a sip of her coffee. "What's it all about? Where do I go from here? You know, little questions like that."

Charley laughed. "Yeah, the easy stuff. Maybe things will get a little clearer when we go down to Cowell's this afternoon." Cowell's was a state park just south of the small town of Felton on a narrow winding road called Highway 9.

"Maybe, but I wouldn't bet on it."

"Of course you wouldn't. You don't bet on anything."

"OK, I wouldn't count on it. How's that?"

"You never know," Charley said. She got up, took Savarna's empty plate from her lap and made her way inside. "Sometimes the answers are right in front of our face, but we just don't listen."

Chapter Five

"Damn," Johnny said, "if we have to keep discarding Mrs. Stephanos's embryos from all these bad PGDs, we aren't going to have much left to work with." PGD or Pre-implantation Genetic Diagnosis was a process that involved the biopsy of a cell from an embryo to tell what the chromosomes were like and if it was genetically normal.

"Not again," Savarna said. "Isn't that the fifth or sixth one?"

"Yeah, but keep the faith. The next one will be perfect."

"There you go," Savarna said, as she quickly observed some Day Two embryos for viability and possible transfer under the microscope. "Never say die."

"Savarna?" Marie's voice came through on the intercom to the front office.

"Yes, Marie."

"Your mother's here and would like to take you to tea on your next break."

"Your mother?" Johnny said. "She hardly ever comes by."

"Tell her I'll be out as soon as I can," Savarna said. "My hands are full at the moment."

"Yeah," Johnny chimed in. "We're trying to keep humanity going in here. Give us a break."

Savarna and Marie laughed.

"I'll let her know you'll be out as soon as you can."

"I'll bet she's got some tall dark handsome guy from India in tow and is waiting to spring him on you."

"Slightly dramatic," Savarna said grinning, "but I wouldn't put it past her."

After another round of evaluations and a barrage of Johnny's sarcasm, Savarna removed her scrubs and journeyed forth to face her determined, pragmatic mother.

"Where is he, Mom?" Savarna said as she entered the front office and her mother rose to greet her.

"Where is who?" her mother replied, looking bewildered as she followed her daughter's scanning gaze.

"Where's the guy you want me to marry?"

The administrative assistant, Marie, kept typing, as if she weren't eavesdropping.

"What?" her mother asked. "Who do you think I am? I'd never think of doing such a thing." Savarna cocked her head to the side, continuing to look accusingly at her mother. "I'd always tell you their background first," her mom explained, "and get your approval before setting up a meeting with any young man."

"So?" Savarna continued, as she gave her mother a reluctant hug and led her towards the front door. "Whoever he is and no matter what he does, I will not meet, let alone marry, anyone."

"Who said anything about marrying or meeting someone? I've got something more important to talk with you about."

* * * *

Within a quarter of an hour, Savarna and her mother were seated in Mira's friend Satya's tea room on El Camino Blvd.

As soon as their chai and small bowls of palak paneer had been served, Savarna's mother said, "You have to have a baby."

Savarna almost spit out the mouthful she'd just taken. "Mom, this is the last time I'm going to tell you this and I'm going to tell you why. I will never get married. If you haven't—"

"I don't care if you get married," her mother interjected. "I don't even care if you have a boyfriend anymore, but you have to have a baby."

Everything stopped in Savarna's head. This didn't make any sense at all. The shock of her mother's statement made her wonder if she'd heard her correctly.

The Last Conception

"Did you say you don't care if I get married?"

Her mother fidgeted in her chair, looked down at her lap and then back at Savarna. "Yes, you heard me right. I don't care anymore if you ever get married or not. Well... I care and wish you would, but... we are running out of time and you need to have a baby."

"Running out of time? I'm only thirty-four. I've got plenty of time, and I'm not even sure I want to have a baby anyway." Her mother glanced away momentarily. "I can't believe what you just said. After all these years and all the pressure, you suddenly don't care if I'm married or not! This is crazy. What's going on?"

Mira took her daughter's hands in hers. "Trust me. I can't explain everything now, but it is imperative that you have a child."

"What are you saying? What brought this on? Are you OK?"

"I'm fine. Never felt better. It has nothing to do with me. It isn't my decision or yours."

"Not my decision? Of course it's my decision, and it's mine alone. You have been meddling in my life for too long. What gives you the right to tell me to have a baby?"

"I'm not trying to tell you what to do. I'm trying to tell you what needs to be done."

"That's enough," Savarna said, sitting straighter in her chair. "I don't know what's gotten into you, but this is crazy. I don't want to hear anymore of this nonsense."

Her mother leaned forward, "But you—"

"No!" Savarna insisted. "No more. I've got to get back to work."

Mira looked suddenly exhausted, as if she'd been walking through knee-deep mud.

"Mom. I love you, but you are freaking me out here, and I've really got to get back." She took her mother's hand as she stood and helped her up. "Let's talk about this some other time, OK?"

Mira made no reply or attempt to say another word on the drive back toward the fertility lab, where her only daughter who could have a child continued to help others carry on their family name, but refused to consider doing the same.

Chapter Six

Johnny, his girlfriend, Vicki, Magdalena, and Savarna made their way through the mass of sweating bodies at the Oakland Coliseum, and were able to squeeze toward the middle, just as Mary J. Blige made her way on stage to a thunderous ovation.

"What did I tell you?" Johnny exclaimed, just after Mary had finished belting out the first set of the evening.

"Fantastic," Savarna yelled, then realized she didn't need to scream since they sat right next to one another. "It's like she knows me inside out and is singing just to me."

"Hey," Magdalena shoved Savarna's shoulder, as she spoke to Johnny. "I've been telling her about MJB for ages, but she never listens to a word I say."

"I guess it just took a man's touch," Johnny joked, "to wake her up to real talent." Savarna laughed. Vicki squeezed Johnny around the waist and kissed him.

"Pleeeease," Magdalena replied, rolling her eyes. "Get real."

"She is really amazing," Savarna said. "Thanks for getting us all tickets."

"No problem," Johnny replied. "Only had to pay a scalper a thousand a piece."

"What?" Vicki and Magdalena both exclaimed simultaneously. Savarna knew he was kidding.

"Yep. Probably the last four tickets available on earth," Johnny said, as the other women caught on.

"You must be rich!" Vicki played along. "I'm sure it won't bother you one bit to buy me a new dress at Chantall's Boutique this weekend and take me to that private island of yours in the Caribbean."

"Don't push the limits now, dear," Johnny mocked. "You know that Sir Richard Branson at Virgin happened to buy the exact same Caribbean island I had my eyes set on, and no other will really do."

"Oh, that's right," Vicki said, batting her long eyelashes. "And that property up in Washington State was already scooped up by your friend Bill Gates."

"That's why I love you." Johnny grinned and brushed his hand through Vicki's black curly hair. He gently tugged on her earlobe. "You're so understanding."

"Hetero's," Magdalena whispered to Savarna. "Give me a break."

"They're just having fun. Lighten up."

"If I lighten up any more, I'll be as white as your girl, what's her name?"

"You mean Charley?"

"You've got other white girlfriends I don't know about?"

"No, but you probably do."

Magdalena started to object but looked away without a reply.

* * * *

As they made their way to get some refreshments and return before the crowd squeezed the life out of them, Johnny put his hand on Savarna's shoulder, leaned down and asked, "What happened with your mom the other day at lunch? You haven't said a word about it."

"I didn't know what to say and you wouldn't believe it if I told you."

"Try me."

They arrived at the bagel concession stand. Magdalena and Vicki stood together in line, while Savarna tried to explain to Johnny what she didn't understand herself.

"And then she says, 'I don't care if you're married anymore, but you have to have a baby.'"

"That's crazy," Johnny said. "After all of these years trying to get you married off."

"That's what I said."

"Something's going on."

"Tell me about it. Hopefully I'll find out something tomorrow when I see my dad."

"You aren't coming in to work?"

"No, no. I'll be there. He asked me to stop by his office afterwards."

"I hate to ask this, but do you think one of them is sick or something?"

"That's what I'm wondering. Guess I'll find out soon enough."

"As far as having a baby, you know I'm always glad to donate to the cause."

Savarna laughed.

"Donate to what cause?" Vicki asked, as she and Magdalena handed their respective dates a bagel and coffee.

Savarna and Johnny grinned.

"Nothing," Johnny said, "just the cause to save mankind."

"You mean womankind," Magdalena corrected.

"Yeah," Johnny said. "Woman, man, your kind, my kind… whatever."

"Whatever?" Magdalena said.

"Come on," Savarna said, grabbing Magdalena by the sleeve. "The concert is about to start!"

* * * *

They couldn't get back to their original location but were pushed to the right of the stage and ended up having a better spot than before.

Song after song struck a chord with Savarna. She found herself crying more than once. When MJB sang "Take Me As I Am," she couldn't help think about Charley. "So take me as I am or have nothing at all…" And the words to "Each Tear" shot straight to her heart. "There's something that I want to say, but I feel like I don't know how. Still I just can't hold it one more day, so I think I let it out."

As Mary J. Blige sang, Savarna was certain she looked right at her when she finished the last line. *You're right*, Savarna promised herself. *I've got to let it out.*

Chapter Seven

The bell rang as Savarna entered her father's store the next afternoon. It was the first specialty foods store he'd opened when she was a little girl, and his office was upstairs.

"Savarna!" Siva Muktananda exclaimed, as she looked up up from the bag of curry powder she was helping a young woman measure. She limped around the corner in her garish green and purple sari, with yellowish-orange hands from the powder, and gave Savarna a long embrace. Being well-proportioned and having no qualms about trying everything in the shop, Mrs. Muktananda had always appeared to be a giant when Savarna first met her as a child. She wore a ton of jewelry—earrings, necklaces, arm and ankle bracelets, and a nose ring—which all clanged together like a brass band as she walked.

"Let me look at you." Siva grinned, placing her hands firmly on Savarna's shoulders. Savarna could feel the perspiration from Mrs. Muktananda's hands through the blue cotton dress shirt she'd worn to work. "You are as beautiful as ever." Siva turned toward the young lady she'd been working with. "This is Mr. Sikand's daughter Savarna." The employee nodded her head and smiled. "I've known her ever since she came up to my knee. And she's smart too." Siva beamed proudly, as if Saverna was her own daughter. "She's a scientist! Savarna, this is Johti."

"Nice to meet you, Johti."

"She started about a week ago," Siva whispered. "I think she'll work out, but they don't make them like they used to."

"I'm sure she'll be great," Savarna assured her. "How is your hip?"

"Oh, same old thing. They say I should get a hip replacement one of these days."

"It can help a lot, like night and day."

"That's what they say. So," Siva said, raising her eyebrows, "enough about my old creaking hips. Any good looking prospects these days? Your mother was telling me about a man just last week who sounded like a dream."

"Papa is expecting me," Savarna quickly replied. "I should go on up."

"Of course, of course. He's so proud of you," Siva said. "Fill me in on your way out."

"I will."

"Promise."

"Always."

* * * *

The stairs up to her father's office groaned with the slightest pressure. She made her way down a hall filled floor to ceiling with boxes of products stacked precariously on either side. All of her father's other stores had plenty of storage. *Why did he refuse to add more space out back and work in such clutter?* she asked herself. It was also as hot as hell in summer, since he'd never put in air-conditioning. When it came to business, her dad had learned how to throw the dice with predictable risks and benefited considerably, but when it concerned his environment he seemed to cling to the familiar and was reluctant to change.

She knocked on the old pine door, which, by its unpainted appearance, no one would know was the entrance to the office of a man who owned four Bay Area Indian Markets and would soon expand into Central California.

"Come in."

She opened the door slowly and peeked around the side. "Papa."

Her father jumped up from his seat. "Savarna! Come in!" He hugged her and kissed both her cheeks. "Here. Here." He pulled the rolling chair away from the front of the desk and motioned for her to sit. She noticed that he had put a cushion on the cold metal chair, which was a great improvement since she'd last stopped by. As she sat, he returned to his seat.

The Last Conception

"Thank you for coming by. I know you are a very busy woman."

"Not any busier than you."

As if on cue, the phone rang. Mr. Sikand looked at the number. "I've got to get this. It will just take a second."

While her father spoke to the caller, in a much louder and more assured voice than he ever did at home, Savarna took a quick survey. The old-fashioned ledgers were still on the shelves, even though her father had been using Excel for years and had a bookkeeper. The photograph on the wall of her parents standing in a crowd a few feet away from Indira Gandhi had so much dust on the glass that all the faces were blurred. The modern stainless steel file cabinets seemed out of place. The moderate-sized window to the right looked out onto the rooftop of the dry cleaner's next door. Thank goodness it was open. She was sure that her father's health had been compromised after all the years he'd spent cooped up inside this claustrophobic office.

She heard her father stop talking and the phone being placed back in its holder.

"So, how are you today?"

"Good. A little tired, but good."

"Tired?"

"I went to a concert last night and got home late."

"I hope it was good and not some hippy hoppy stuff."

"It was actually quite good. You haven't heard of Mary J. Blige, have you?"

"Of course," he grinned, "Your mother saw her on Oprah once and said she had heart."

Savarna laughed. "She's got heart all right and a great voice."

"Not as good as yours I bet."

"What? I can't sing on key for the life of me. You're thinking of Chitra."

"Chitra? Oh yeah. Well, you have a lovely voice too."

"So, what's going on? Mom said some crazy things the other day."

Mr. Sikand suddenly looked uncomfortable, as if he'd just been shot up with speed and couldn't sit still. He fiddled with some papers, picked up his pen and put it down again.

"Dad?"

"She wasn't saying anything crazy at all," he said, clearing his throat and looking up at his daughter. "We are in complete agreement. You need to have a baby."

The added confirmation from her father for this seemingly sudden and bizarre baby fixation by her parents sent her mind spinning in a thousand directions. If she'd have glanced in a mirror at that moment, she would have seen the face of someone displaying all the classic signs of shock--her mouth dropped, her eyes widened and her skin turned ashen.

"We would prefer you were married, but you aren't getting any younger, and we can't wait," her father continued. "It's no fault of Chitra's that she can't have children, since all her um... organs were removed with the cancer. But you, you are healthy, of childbearing age and we've waited long enough."

Slowly coming to, Savarna responded to the astonishing statements her father was throwing at her. "Childbearing age? You've waited long enough? What on earth has gotten into you? You've never been as bad as Mom has about me getting married and now, out of the blue, you are both insisting that I have a baby! Who's put you two up to this? Is it Grandma?" Davidia shook his head. "Then stop telling me what to do and give me some answers here."

"In a way, it does have to do with your grandmother and with her parents and their parents and your great-great-great grandparents. One generation after another has continued our traditions and carried on our heritage. You are our last hope. It hasn't been easy for us to see you remain single for such a long time, and you know your mother has been determined to find you a husband. It's not just because we want you to be happy, but so you could also have children. But now... we finally realized that for whatever reason, you may not ever get married, and it is vital that you carry on our lineage and have a child." He leaned forward. "Of course, we'd still prefer you get married and hope you will soon, but time is running out."

"Dad, I'm only thirty-four, so I've got another five or six years, and I'm not sure if I ever want to bring a child into this world, especially all by myself. I've seen a lot of single parents, and it is by far the most difficult thing to ever do, to raise a child by yourself, even if you have

The Last Conception

family around to help. I'm not in a committed relationship right now, at least not from my perspective and--"

"Yes, yes. I understand. That's why we think you should go ahead and get pregnant. We will provide everything you need and hire someone to help out while you're at work. If anybody knows how to make a baby, surely it is you."

"Of course I know how, but it changes everything in your life. Nothing is ever the same. Even if I had someone twenty-four hours a day to help, I'd still be thinking about them and worrying about them all the time. And if I and I mean I—not you, Mom, Grandmother, or anyone else—ever decide to have a child, I don't want it being raised by other people. That would be my job and joy."

"However you want to do it would be fine with us, but please consider it carefully. As you said, it does affect everything, and your child will affect more than you'll ever know. As far as being in a relationship... there is no problem. It's just a matter of time until some guy sees the precious diamond that you are and sweeps you and your baby off your feet."

"Dad—" The phone rang again and her father quickly picked it up, lifting his finger up to Savarna, signaling her to hold on just a minute.

"Yes, Mr. Bennelli. The escrow on that site is supposed to close in about two more weeks. We'll be moving in within a month and are very excited to have your support." Mr. Sikand smiled at Savarna. "No, we will not put up any large signs that would interfere with your business," he said, shaking his head slightly side to side. "I'm glad you approve. Can we meet next week? Good. Good. I'll call you soon. Goodbye."

Mr. Sikand hung up. "Sorry. You were saying?"

The phone rang again. Davidia raised his shoulders and hands, implying he had no choice; he had to answer it again. He placed his hand on the receiver to pick it up, but Savarna placed her hand on his and stopped him.

"No. Not now," she said. "I'm gay. I'll never marry a 'nice man' and have no interest in doing so. I like women and always have. It has nothing to do with you or Mom or anything you've done or not done. I've been afraid to tell you for years. I wasn't sure what you'd say or do. I still don't know why I haven't told you before. I always figured you knew, but apparently I figured wrong. So, there it is. Out in the open." She spread her arms outwards and sat back to wait for the onslaught of anger, judgment and rejection. It never came.

"Well," her father said, after a long pause. "That will complicate things."

"That's all?"

"No," he said quickly and took her hand in his. "I'm really glad you told me, but you have to give me a moment. I really had no idea. I just thought you were stubborn and waiting for Mr. Right."

"Dad, you're the only Mr. Right in my life."

Mr. Sikand blinked and wiped a tear away with the sleeve of his permanent-pressed white dress shirt.

"Let's take this slowly. Let me tell your mother, OK?"

"Please do. It's been exhausting keeping this from you. I'm sorry it took me so long. I don't know what I was afraid of."

"Better late than never, as they say."

"I don't know about that, Dad. With some things, never is the best."

"As far as what we were talking about before, 'never' is out of the question. I'm not saying anything else right now. Just think about it, and I'll let your little newsflash sink in." He grinned with his attempt at making a joke.

"You've got it, Babba."

"Don't 'Babba' me, my little Savarna-ji."

They rose, went around the side of the desk and embraced. Her father walked her to the door. A father's love cut through the dingy office and pervaded his first-born daughter's heart. A smile lit up her face, as she turned and left.

Mr. Sikand went back to his desk, picked up the phone and dialed.

"Mira, it's going to be harder than we ever dreamed, but there's still hope."

* * * *

She had just finished writing in her journal, to make sure she didn't forget anything that had transpired and was sitting down to have a spinach salad at the beautiful glass table she'd gotten from Kia last month, when the phone rang. The meeting with her father, on top of working a long day, had worn her out. She let it ring and enjoyed another mouthful. She loved the lemon-tahini dressing she'd discovered and had a habit of drenching her salads beyond reason with the yummy concoction.

"Savarna? Savarna?" her mother's voice echoed on the answering machine. "Please pick up the phone. We've got to talk. Savarna? Savaaaarna? Ahhh!" She hung up.

The next call would come within ten minutes, she predicted, as she kept on chewing. She didn't get her stubbornness from out of the blue. Her mother had it in spades.

As she was rinsing her bowl and placing it in the dishwasher, the phone rang again. Knowing her mother wouldn't stop until she picked up, she grabbed the phone off the stand and went to sit on the love seat she'd recently had re-upholstered. It had belonged to her parents and been a gift when she first moved in.

"Hi, Mom. I just got out of the shower and was starting dinner."

"Your father told me everything."

"And?"

"Is this some kind of phase or something?"

Savarna had expected as much.

"No, Mom, it's not a phase, but it's definitely something."

"How long has this been going on? I mean, how long have you known?"

"A long, long time. It didn't just happen overnight."

She heard her mother sigh and tried to prepare herself for whatever came next. She had a feeling that her mother had known for some time but hadn't dared ask.

"Are you, um, are you 'involved' with anyone now?"

"Yes. I've been going out with Magdalena and Charley and—"

"You mean there's more than one?!"

She kept herself from laughing loudly. She knew her mother had no tact about this kind of thing and would want to know everything.

"Yes, but it's only these two. What do you think, we go around having big orgies or something?"

"Savarna! Of course not."

"What I started to say, Mom, is that they are both great people, but very different. And I don't mean weird different. I'm not sure where I'm at with Magdalena, but Charley wants to seriously settle down and commit."

"Well, there you go. You should definitely choose Charley."

"Mom, you don't even know how I feel. How can you judge so quickly?"

"It's just common sense, and why does this woman have a man's name?"

"It's short for Charlemagne."

"Then why doesn't she use her given name?"

"She does. Just her close friends call her Charley."

"That doesn't sound proper. You should—"

"Mom, stop with the 'shoulds.' How are you doing with all this? I tried to tell you at your birthday party, but—"

"I have to confess that it's not a total surprise."

"Really?"

"When your daughter doesn't go out with any men since college, doesn't ever mention a man, and gets a sparkle in her eye whenever she talks about her girl 'friends,' it doesn't take a genius to figure something's not right. I mean, not as it should be. I mean—"

"That's OK, Mom. I know what you mean."

"I think I've always put it out of my mind because it meant you wouldn't get married, have children, and carry on the family name. I wanted it to be different and hoped you could somehow change."

"Mom, I can still get married, have a child, if I choose to, and carry on the family name.

"Yes, I finally realized that you don't need to have a man for all that, but isn't it easier?"

"No, not if you're me."

"I'm not sure how to tell your grandmother about this. I doubt she'd understand."

"Grandma is a lot smarter than you give her credit for. Just because she's never left her hometown doesn't mean she's dumb."

"I wasn't saying she is. I'm just not sure how to tell her that you might not have a baby, at least any time soon."

"What is so important about having a baby? It seems like you and

Dad have become infected with some 'must have baby… must have baby' gene. I don't get it."

"It's your destiny."

"My destiny? How do you know what my destiny is?"

"Trust me. I know."

"Well, let someone else fulfill this destiny thing. I'm not interested."

"There is nobody else. Your sister might have been able, but—"

"Having a baby has nothing to do with destiny, Mom. It is a natural drive that people have to procreate and keep the species going, and thank God, most people now have the choice of when and if they want to have children."

"You're wrong. In this case, it is your destiny."

"If you insist."

"I do."

"Anything else you want to know? I've got to get back to work for a meeting."

"Would you like to bring Charlemagne over for dinner sometime?"

"You want to meet Charley?"

"If she's serious about settling down or whatever you call it when two women, you know… have a situation."

"Move in together?"

"Yes. Then we'd like to meet her."

"Maybe. I'll check it out next time I see her, but if she does come over you have to promise to keep the baby and destiny stuff to yourself, OK?"

"Yes, dear."

"I've got to go, Mom."

"Call me."

"Mom, of course I'll call you. If I don't, you'll be ringing day and night."

Her mother laughed. "Don't ever forget that I love you."

"Love you too. And thanks."

"Thanks for what?"

"For not freaking out."

"Well, I am a little…"

"Mom, stop while you're ahead."

"Bye, Savarna."

"Bye, Mom."

Her parents' newfound baby fetish was most peculiar and was starting to get on Savarna's nerves. She couldn't figure out if it had something to do with them aging and worrying about having grandchildren, Indian tradition of carrying on the family name, or a combination of both. The pressure to get married year after year had already taken its toll. Now this. Pretty soon nothing would be a surprise. For all she knew, the next step would be for them to offer to hire some gigolo to personally "get the job done."

Chapter Eight

"Come on, it will be fun." Savarna read the message from Magdalena that was waiting on her email when she got home late from the ethics committee meeting at work. "You can't say no to this," it said. "I'll get you home early and put you to bed myself (hopefully). I promise! Somebody said Holly Near might even show up at the party as a surprise guest! You've avoided me all week. It's time to show up and have a good time. There's more to life than work and all your family drama. Live it up a little. We won't be around forever."

As usual, Luscious had greeted her at the door with some welcoming meows, followed her around the house, and jumped up onto her lap as soon as she'd sat down at the computer. She rubbed Luscious behind the ears and hugged her to her chest. The cat's purr was as loud as a Harley motorcycle being revved up at a stop sign.

"She is so persistent." Savarna exclaimed out loud to the cat. "Doesn't she get the message?" She didn't know exactly why, but something had shifted in the last few weeks. Perhaps it had been her talk with Charley in Santa Cruz or her parents' behavior of late. Whatever it was, she no longer saw any point in having a good time just for the sake of it. It wasn't always "good" either. Everyone tried too hard to look happy, even when they weren't. And even though they didn't speak about it much, she was certain that Magdalena was seeing anybody she could lay her hands on and didn't really care that much about their relationship one way or another, other than for sex.

"I'll have to pass. Thank you for the invite. I'm sure it will be a blast. All the best, Savarna." She sent this to-the-point email back to

Magdalena, gently put Luscious on the floor, and got ready for bed. The cat followed her from room to room and jumped up on the bathroom sink when she brushed her teeth. Luscious always got great pleasure from watching the water twirl around in the sink before it made its descent down the drain. She went back into her office and decided to check her email once more before calling it a night. Magdalena had already replied.

"Your loss. There are plenty of women dying to go. I always think of you first. Not surprised though. Give me a call when you've come to your senses and realize you'll never find anyone that is as into you as I am. By the way, Charley isn't all you think she is. From what I've heard, she's about as much fun as watching it rain."

I like to watch it rain, Savarna thought. Savarna sent Charley a quick message, "Thinking of you. Goodnight," and then turned off her computer.

She made her way to bed and got under the covers. Luscious leaped onto the thin silk comforter Savarna's grandmother had given her years ago, and made her way up the spread, where she collapsed on Savarna's chest and promptly purred. Savarna could feel the cat's weight and warmth. Its whiskers tickled her nose.

"You'll never leave me for someone else or insist I have a baby, will you?" she said to her cat. "I wish humans weren't so complicated."

The next thing she heard was her alarm. It was five in the morning. Time to get up and help people have babies.

Chapter Nine

"Are you ready for this?" Savarna asked Charley. They sat in the car in her parents' driveway.

"Yes. I've been ready for a long time. Are you?"

"No, but I never will be."

Charley grabbed the bowl of cranberry salad she'd made from the back seat. It was one of her family's favorites. She hoped they would like it.

"Remember—" Savarna began, but was quickly interrupted.

"I know. I know. No kissing, hugging, or touching in front of your parents. Don't argue with your dad about politics, and don't be offended if your mom acts like she's not listening, because she probably is."

"Wow, did I really say all that?"

"That's only half of it."

Savarna had to laugh. Charley was the calm and collected one, whereas Savarna felt like she was back in high school about to give a speech to the entire student body and discovered she'd forgotten to put on her clothes.

Savarna knocked and opened the door. "Mom? Dad? We're here!"

Her mother came running with her father close behind.

"Savarna!" her mother said and gave her a big hug. Her father followed suit. Then they both turned toward the lady holding a dish with some pink concoction inside. "And this must be Charlemagne?" her father asked.

"Mom, Dad, this is…"

"Please, call me Charley," Charley said, offering her hand.

Savarna's parents both took her hand and gave her a hug. "Welcome to our home," Mr. Sikand said.

"And what is this wonderful looking dish you brought?" Mrs. Sikand asked.

"It's been a family recipe for generations and is one of my favorites. We've never had a name for it. We just call it a cranberry salad. It needs to stay frozen until just before it's served. Is there room in your freezer?"

"Right this way, young lady," Mrs. Sikand said and turned to show her the way.

A second before she followed Mrs. Sikand, Charley turned and whispered to Savarna, "No hugging?" Savarna raised her shoulders and shook her head in disbelief.

After Mrs. Sikand had led Charley to the kitchen, Savarna's father put his arm around his daughter. "She seems like a nice girl, I mean woman."

"She is, Dad."

"So, you really like her?" he asked, as he led Savarna to the living room and poured her a cup of tea. She nodded. "And you're not seeing anyone else, right?" Savarna nodded again. "So…" he cleared his throat. "You think she may be the one for you or your special friend or something like that?"

"Yes." Savarna smiled. She had to restrain herself from laughing out loud. She understood how hard he was trying to be accepting and say the right things. It's not every day that an Indian-American woman brings home her girlfriend to meet her conservative, traditional Indian parents.

"Well… if it makes you happy… if *she* makes you happy…"

"*She* does, Dad." Savarna kissed her father on the cheek. "She makes me very happy, and she knows what she wants. She's a rock."

"Does she know if she wants a baby?"

"Dad! Come on! We don't even live together yet. Stop this baby nonsense."

"It's not nonsense, and what do you mean 'yet' about living together?"

"Davidia!" Mira exclaimed, walking into the living room with her arm around Charley. "Charlemagne, I mean Charley, has an art exhibit at Rhiannon's in Menlo Park. It sounds marvelous. And her mother's a lawyer."

"You know all of that, just from going to the kitchen and back?" Davidia grinned.

"And her father is a policeman. Poor girl's parents got divorced, but she says she sees them both often, and they all get along. Here, here, let me get you some tea." Mrs. Sikand poured some steaming tea into a small cup with intricate designs around its border and handed it to Charley.

"Well, I can top that," Mr. Sikand smiled. "Savarna and Ms. Burnell, I mean Charley, are going to live together real soon."

Charley almost spit out her tea. "We... we are?" She looked at Savarna, who was trying to hide without hiding. "I mean... yes, we are."

"That's not exactly what I..."

"That's wonderful," Mrs. Sikand said, as she gave her daughter a hug.

"But Mom... Dad... doesn't this sort of thing go against all your religious beliefs? I mean, I'm not trying to put a damper on anything, but I'm a little confused."

"Please," Mr. Sikand said, "have a seat." They all sat, carefully taking sips of tea, then placing their cups on the coffee table. Davidia and Mira sat in the love seat and Savarna and Charley sat opposite on the orange velvet couch. "Let me explain. You're right, Savarna, we have strong religious beliefs and adhere to our faith in everything we do. Marriage is among the most important and holy of our laws. Normally, we don't think it is right for people to just, as you say, 'live together,' let alone two women... at least not as partners or mates or whatever you call it."

"Here it comes," Savarna whispered to Charley. "I knew it was too good to be true."

"But—" Her father raised his head and looked at his wife, then back at his daughter and Charley— "In these circumstances, there are traditions that take precedence and over-ride whatever we may or may not believe. Raising a child with two parents is difficult enough, but to try it on your own.... We want you to have all of the support you can, and if the two of you being together will help that process or be the catalyst for you to have a child, then we are all for it. We are willing to sacrifice our personal values for the greater good. We—"

"Sacrifice," Savarna almost shouted. "Us being together is not a 'sacrifice,' it's a choice and a privilege. I love this woman and would whether you okayed it or not. I thought you were genuinely happy for *me*, not some 'greater good' or some ridiculous tradition you keep throwing in my face."

That was the first time Charley had ever heard Savarna say she loved her in public, let alone to her parents. It was rare enough in private.

Mrs. Sikand took her daughter's hand. "We *are* happy for you. We are happy for both of you. Your father is saying that it would take us longer to accept your arrangement and probably would have been more difficult for us to understand if it wasn't for the situation we find ourselves in."

"What 'situation'?" Savarna asked. "I'm getting sick of hearing about some special circumstance, as if I'm any part of it."

"But you are part of it," Mr. Sikand said. "You have no idea how big a part you play."

Just then the doorbell rang, and Chitra and Mike entered. Everyone stood as Savarna's sister and her husband made their way to the living room. Greetings, handshakes, and hugs were exchanged.

"So," Chitra said to Charley, "you're the beautiful woman who's stolen my sister's heart?"

Charley's cheeks reddened. Savarna playfully pushed Chitra on the shoulder. "Stop it," she said. "You're embarrassing her and…" She nodded towards her parents.

"They're OK. Let them do what they've got to do," Chitra replied. "If they can't see something good when it's right in front of them, that's their problem."

"What do you mean, we can't see?" her mother said. "We can see just fine. Charley is a sweet girl, and did you know her mother is a lawyer?"

"Isn't dinner about ready?" Mr. Sikand suddenly stated, his eyes darting towards the kitchen.

"Yes, yes," Mrs. Sikand exclaimed. "Let's have dinner." She motioned for everyone to follow her to the dining room. "Charley brought the most delightful dish. It's called a cranbury salad or something like that."

"Cranberry salad, Mom," Savarna corrected.

"Whatever it is, it's good. I took a little taste before we put it in the freezer. It's tart and sweet at the same time. Sort of like a good curry, but frozen."

Mike came alongside Savarna and said, "She's cute. You've got good taste."

"Yes, I do," Savarna replied, while her mother and Charley walked ahead. *And she tastes good too*, Savarna thought. A warm grin spread across her lips.

* * * *

"*What is that sound?*" Savarna wondered. She lay half-asleep snuggled up next to Charley, who had stayed the night, after a delicious dinner and long conversation with her family about everything and anything, except getting pregnant. "There it is again." She opened her eyes and realized it was her cell phone ringing. She looked at the bedside clock. "Who's calling at 3:30 a.m.? I hope this isn't some prank." Her hand found the insistent ringing phone. "Hello… What?!... When?... Where is she?... It will be OK, Dad. I'll be right there."

Charley was sitting up. She put both of her hands on Savarna's shoulders. "What's wrong?"

"Mom," Savarna said rising and running to her closet to grab some clothes. "She's had a heart attack."

"Oh no. I'm so sorry. Is she…"

"She's stable. That's all Dad could say."

"Let me come with you. Hold on a minute." Charley grabbed her pants by the side of the bed and started to get dressed.

"No, not now," Savarna insisted.

Charley followed her to the door. "Are you sure you've got enough juice in your car? Do you want to take mine?"

"I've got more than enough. It's been charging for five hours already." She quickly kissed Charley. "I'll call you."

As Savarna started to leave, Charley grabbed her by the shoulder and turned her around. "Are you sure you don't want me to come?"

"Yes. Yes. I'm fine. I promise I'll call."

Charley could see Savarna's lower lip quivering and her body slightly shaking, but knew it would be useless to argue. She kissed Savarna again. "Don't forget, I'm here. You don't have to go through this alone."

"I know. I've got to go."

She dashed to the garage, unplugged the car, opened the automatic door and sped towards the hospital. "Come on, Mom," she pleaded. "Hold on. Don't do anything stupid." Any thought of her mother dying was quickly thrown in the garbage bin of her mind. She only had room for hope. She couldn't begin to imagine a world without her mother in it.

* * * *

Saint Mary Margaret's Catholic Hospital looked like any other that night. It stood three stories high, sprawled out on two acres, with rows of mostly empty parking spaces near the front entrance. A monstrous brightly lit cross adorned the north wing and could be seen from all directions. Lampposts along the sidewalk provided spotlights for Savarna to find her way to a stage she had no desire to appear upon. The last time she'd been at Santa Mary Margaret's was fifteen years ago when she'd had an emergency appendectomy. The doctors, nurses, aides, and staff had all been wonderful, for the most part, but it was still a hospital. Unlike her lab, she had little control over what happened inside these walls.

She found the Cardiac Care Unit and saw her father through the large window of her mother's room, sitting listlessly, as if he were half dead himself. Without asking for permission, Savarna strode past the nurses' station and walked in. Her mother was not on a respirator but was breathing on her own. That was an instant relief. All of the other usual apparatus for such situations were in use. Two different lines had been inserted; one subclavian IV just below her neck, and another intravenous drip in her arm. A tube of oxygen ran from a wall socket to the mask over her nose and mouth, and five different wires from the heart monitor were attached to pads stuck on her chest and side.

"Dad?"

He looked up, wiped a tear from his cheek, then stood and hugged his daughter.

The Last Conception

"What happened? What have the doctors said?"

"Shhhh." He nodded at his wife, then took Savarna's hand and led her outside to the waiting room.

Her father held tight to Savarna's hand as he tried to explain. "She seemed fine. We talked about dinner and meeting Ms. Burnell, I mean Charley. I told her I thought your friend was too liberal but had a good heart and seemed like a nice person. And she obviously cares about you. I'm not sure what—"

"Dad. Mom. What happened to Mom?"

"Yes. Yes. Just before we went to sleep she said she was very tired. Now, you know your mom. She never ever seems tired, let alone says that she is. I didn't pay much attention to it then. I was tired myself. I wish I had said something or asked why." Davidia looked out the window, then back at Savarna and continued. "About an hour after we went to sleep. Maybe it was an hour and ten minutes. I'm not sure."

"It's OK, Dad."

"Yes, well, anyway. I was half-asleep when she said, 'I can't breathe. Help.' At first I didn't know what she was talking about, but as soon as I turned on the light I could see her holding her chest and her eyes... I've never seen her look so frightened! I knew something was wrong. That's when I called 911."

Savarna put her arm around her father's shoulders. "You did just the right thing, Dad. She's going to be OK." Savarna wasn't as sure as she sounded. "What have the doctors said?"

"They said it was precarious, and they would know more in the next 24 hours."

"Did you call Chitra and Mike?"

"They're on their way."

"Dad, look at me." Mr. Sikand raised his head. "Who is the strongest woman in the world?"

"Your mom."

"And who says that nothing and nobody can keep her down?"

"Mira."

"And who has survived living with you all these years?"

Mr. Sikand grinned and nodded.

"She's got to get through this," she was telling herself, as much as her father. "None of us can cook as good as she can and we sure as hell can't swear at you in Malayalam."

Mira opened her eyes the next morning. Davidia was in the chair immediately next to her bed, snoring. On the other side were Chitra and Mike, propping one another up, shoulder to shoulder. Savarna and Charlemagne were standing together talking just outside the door to her room. Savarna looked in, saw her mother's eyes were open and rushed in. Charley was close behind.

"Mom? Mom? How are you feeling?"

The sudden movement and question awoke the rest of the family. Davidia stood and hugged his wife, with tears wetting both their faces. Chitra and Mike pulled their chairs closer.

"I'm fine. Don't make such a fuss."

"Mother," Savarna admonished. "There's nothing 'fine' about a heart attack."

"Oh, so that's what it was. No wonder it felt like I'd been struck by lightning. What have the doctors said?"

"Doctor Lopez says you need to rest. They're doing more tests later today to ascertain your condition," Chitra said.

"What caused all of this? I've cut way down on fried foods and walk everywhere. My doctor said my blood pressure was perfect the last time I saw him."

"It could be anything, Mom," Savarna said. "It may have nothing to do with what you've done or not done."

"I hope it wasn't my cranberry salad," Charley said.

Everyone laughed.

"Mira," Davidia said. "They don't know your condition yet. This could be very serious. You should rest and take it easy."

"I understand." Mira lifted her hand and stroked Davidia's cheek. "That's why we should tell them now. We can't wait."

"You're going to be fine."

"I hope so, but just in case."

Mr. and Mrs. Sikand seemed to continue conversing without saying any words out loud. Mira nodded towards the girls, then back at Davidia. They both nodded in agreement.

"Girls," Mr. Sikand addressed his daughters. "There's something we've got to tell you."

"Whatever it is can wait," Savarna said. "Mom's in no condition to—"

"No, it can't wait," her mother replied.

"Mike, Charlemagne," Davidia said. "Would you mind waiting outside?"

Mike and Charley looked at their partners and then one another. "No problem Mr. Sikand," Mike said. "We'll get everyone coffee."

"Thank you," Mr. Sikand said. He closed the sliding door behind them and returned to his spot at the side of the bed. Savarna took Mike's seat next to her sister. "We've been trying to explain, Savarna, without revealing any secrets until it was time, why you need to have a baby."

"Oh, my God," Savarna exclaimed and started to stand. "Not this again."

"Sit down," her father insisted. "It's not at all what you think." Savarna sat and shook her head in disbelief. "This doesn't involve you alone," he continued. "There is an entire faith whose very existence depends on you continuing our teacher's lineage."

"Dad," Chitra said, "this is weird. You're freaking us out."

"He's right," Mira said quietly. "Savarna is the last woman who can continue the family tree that started with our great teacher thousands of years ago."

"Mom," Savarna said, "it's just me. I'm not anyone special."

"You're wrong. You are the only one left," her mother countered. "Through no fault of her own, Chitra cannot carry a child. Bless her heart." Savarna put her hand on Chitra's, as they both teared up. "And as you know, both of your uncle's wives and daughters, your cousins Radha and Shiva, perished in the tsunami. That leaves you, Savarna, as the only remaining family member who can carry forth the lineage by having a child."

"What lineage are you talking about?" Savarna asked. "It's just our family."

"No, it's not," her father said. "Our family is special. Your ancestors are special. They have carried on the generations since our founder's marriage. This is not just a matter of family pride or honor. It is literally keeping the blood of our faith living and present. There is no other faith that can trace this kind of lineage back to its core, at least not one that has ever made it known publicly."

"You know that pilgrimage your father and I make every year?" The girls nodded. "Who do you think those people are? Why do you think we've never told anyone else about it?"

"Do you realize what would happen if anyone discovered our secret?" their father exclaimed, shaking his head. "It would be a zoo, or they'd send us away and say we were delusional."

That's why there are only a few people who know, and we've taken an oath to keep it that way," Mrs. Sikand added.

"You're right," Savarna said, rubbing her hands on her jeans. "They would say you are delusional, and who would blame them? You can't really expect us to believe this, do you?"

"Whether you believe it or not," her father replied, "doesn't change the reality. You are the last in the bloodline, and it is up to you to follow your religious duty. Not for yourself, but for those of us who have kept this a secret and believe that the Great Master's blood flows in your veins and that of your offspring."

"If this is true," Chitra said, "and I don't see how it could be, but if it were, you have no right to put this kind of pressure on Savarna. If, when, and how to have a child is a personal choice and not something that can be imposed by others."

"In most cases," her mother said, "I would totally agree, but this is not an ordinary situation."

"Mom, you're going to be fine," Savarna said. "If you are doing this in any way as some kind of crazy scheme to try to give us hope or something, because you're afraid you might die, then just drop it."

Mr. Sikand looked at Mira and swallowed a sigh. "This is no scheme, as you say. Yes, the doctors said they weren't sure yet, but she'll be fine." He squeezed Mira's hand.

Mira smiled at her husband, then turned towards her children. "We can prove everything. We'll have your grandmother come and tell you in person."

"Grandmother has never left her hometown, Mom, let alone India," Chitra exclaimed, "and even if she did, that wouldn't prove anything."

"It's not what she would say that will show you the truth," Mrs.

The Last Conception

Sikand said calmly. "It's what she'll bring."

* * * *

After their daughters and their respective partners had left the hospital and there were no nurses or other staff in the room, Mira asked Davidia, "Do you think they believe us?"

"No," he replied, as he took Mira's hand in his. "Did you believe it when my mother first told you?" Mira shook her head. "And that was under much better circumstances."

"It didn't take me very long," Mira sighed. "If there was one thing I was certain about you from the very start, it was that you never lied, and that was in large part because you grew up with someone who did the same, your mother."

"That's true. She doesn't lie. I don't recall a single time in my entire life when she has not told the truth."

"Or kept it to herself."

"Yes," Davidia grinned. "She, we, obviously have our secrets, but she only revealed them when the time required it, just like now."

"Was this a good time? Should we have waited?"

"When would the right time be, my sweet? And what if… nothing will… but if you… you know what I mean."

"Yes."

"Then it would have been even more difficult, if not impossible."

"Maybe you're right. She must think we're crazy."

"Not any more so than you thought about my mother. Remember when you told me what she'd said and that you didn't want to say anything bad about her, but you thought she might be a little 'misguided'?"

"Like it was yesterday. I must admit, I thought she was a little loopy at first, but then you confirmed and agreed with what she'd told me. I thought I had gone out of my head and wondered what kind of family I'd gotten myself mixed up with."

They both grinned with the memory.

"It took awhile for me to really understand," Mira said.

"Yes, it took a little convincing, but you came around in a big way."

"I didn't have any choice. It was only me and your brothers who were left."

"You always had a choice, Mira. Even knowing what you came to know, didn't mean that you had to. Nobody, including me, in fact especially me, would ever force you to do such a thing."

"I know that, darling. It was never a question or doubt. I always wanted to have children long before I knew about the bloodline. I always wanted to have *your* children."

Mira and Davidia squeezed each other's aging fingers tightly and sighed.

Chapter Ten

Trying to juggle work and coordinate her mother's care at home over the following weeks with Chitra and her father was taking a toll on Savarna. Thank God her mom had survived, and with medication, exercise, and some relaxation classes, the doctors said she could live another forty years, more or less. Savarna saw that if she didn't find a way to mellow out herself she was going to end up just like her mother, but at a much younger age. She seriously thought about joining her mom in some of the mindfulness-based stress reduction classes that the doctor had "strongly recommended" for Mrs. Sikand.

* * * *

"Yeah, baby," Johnny said, "my favorite task: sperm separation."

Johnny was referring to couples that chose to have gender selection by having the lab separate the sperm, which took out the unhealthy sperm and other unnecessary matter in the semen before insemination. The process was usually seventy-five percent successful in determining the sex of the child, and the large majority that requested the procedure had it done to increase the odds that they had a boy.

"Come on," Savarna chided. "Be a man about it."

"That's the whole point, isn't it?" he replied.

"Yes, and that's what's wrong with it."

"Lighten up, you man-hater." Johnny said, referring to a long-running joke that had gone on between them for years. When they first met, Johnny thought any woman who was attracted to another woman automatically hated men. It took awhile for him to understand that there was no correlation between sexual preference and liking or disliking the opposite sex.

"How can people do that?"

"It's only a bunch of sperm," Johnny replied, as he took a small syringe and emptied the contents onto his slide. "They'd just die out in a few minutes anyway or be discarded. It's not like it's an embryo or anything."

"I don't see the difference. You're still going along with whole idea that having a boy is better."

They had been having this discussion for quite some time, but it had intensified in the last year or two, as more and more couples were coming to their clinic and asking them to use sperm or embryos that would only produce boys. Their recent monthly ethics meeting had gone on late into the evening. Some of the doctors, embryologists, and administrators on staff didn't have any problem with sperm separation but were dead set against embryo selection or using only embryos that were male. Savarna understood the differentiation, but regarded both procedures as unethical.

Others had argued that there was a huge difference. That had set off an hour-long tirade from those in attendance about the inequality of women and men in other countries, such as the lack of girls and women in male-dominated locales (due to infanticide and/or selective abortions) and the education and privilege often given to boys and not girls in many paternalistic cultures. In general, embryologists are against sex selection and all of the reasons why were pontificated, argued, and debated during their meeting. Others said that people would just start going to another clinic that provided sex-selection if they were turned down at theirs.

"No, I'm not," Johnny replied, as he looked through the lens of his microscope. "Do you really want to go over all this again, right now?"

"No, sorry." Savarna sighed. She was double-checking to see how many of Ms. Moning's eggs were fertilized. Ms. Moning was a single parent who already had a five-year-old adopted son and was giving the biological route one more shot. "I've been a little on edge."

"You can say that again. Wait, no, don't say that again." He carefully washed the sperm in the enclosed container with the organic cleaning fluids. "How's your mom today?"

The Last Conception

"A hundred percent better than last week but we're still running around like headless chickens to make sure she's getting low-salt, low-cholesterol meals, and taking her back and forth to all her doctors, physical therapy, and relaxation classes. She's always done the cooking at home and Dad doesn't have a clue, bless his heart."

"Maybe you should join her for one of those classes."

"I can't. I barely have time to drop her off and pick her up."

"Ever heard about asking for help?"

"I can't impose on someone else to pick her up when Chitra or Dad can't and I can't stick her in a taxi."

"No, but I'd be happy to cover for you while you do."

"Well, now, that's an idea."

"A pretty good one, if I say so myself."

"I might take you up on that."

"Speaking of needing help." Johnny brought the lens into clearer focus. "Did I tell you that my niece moved in with me last weekend?"

"What?" Savarna sat up and turned to look Johnny's way. "No, you didn't. At least, I don't think so. I've been so preoccupied."

"Well, there you go." He turned to speak more directly. "You know about my sister?"

Savarna nodded. Johnny had told her all about his sister's struggle with addiction over the years and how worried he was about his niece. He'd had her stay with him as often as possible.

"Social services finally did it. They said she's unfit to raise a child and were going to put Yvette in a foster home. I told them she could live with me. They've been doing all of the home visits and background checks and finally said it would work. Supposedly, it's temporary, but I've got a feeling…"

"If I wasn't all gowned up, I'd march over there and give you a big hug."

"It's no big deal." Johnny turned back to his microscope.

"It's a huge freaking deal. You're going to be a father for that child and I can't think of a better one in the world." Savarna swiveled her chair around to face him. "You just say the word, Johnny-boy, and Charley and I will be glad to hang out with Yvette."

"Thanks. That means a lot. Did you say Charley and you?"

"Yeah," Savarna said through her mask. "She's sort of moved in over the last week."

Johnny turned back around to face Savarna. "Talk about big deals. How'd this happen?"

"Oh, you know." Savarna mumbled and acted like she was still focusing on her work, though she was completely engaged in sharing her news. "Charley's been great helping me out with my mom, and it's been more convenient for her to just stay overnight. She's been bringing a few things from home to make it easier."

"A few things? Such as..."

"Oh, you know, some clothes, personal stuff, a bit of food."

"Any cooking supplies, pictures, or books?"

"Yeah, a few."

"OK," Johnny said. He chuckled. "It's a done deal. When a woman brings over her frying pan and hangs her clothes in your closet, she's moved in. Whether you know it or not. Believe me, I know how that goes."

Savarna cocked her head to the side. "Maybe. It's OK with me."

"Well... talk about congratulations. It looks like they're in order for you as well."

"Thanks. It looks like I've got a couple live ones here." She was looking at two one-to-two grade healthy embryos. "Don't you think it's about time we introduced your friends over there to mine?"

* * * *

Charley had moved in. It wasn't as slow or as gradual as she had told Johnny. They'd talked about it for quite some time, and Charley had been making hints and insinuations for over a year. "Whenever you're ready," she'd said. When everything hit the fan with Savarna's mother, Savarna welcomed the support and change. Not to say that they weren't having their moments. Adjusting to another life form in her space was not as easy as she'd anticipated or hoped. There were new habits, preferences, schedules, and personal intrusions that she and Luscious experienced and sometimes complained about. Charley liked to leave her dishes in the sink in the morning and wash everything in the evening, after she'd been working at her studio. Savarna cleaned up the table immediately after any use and liked everything to be in its place. It gave her a sense of security, safety, and control. Charley was more laid back and didn't seem to need to manipulate her environment or surroundings as much as Savarna did. Then there was the shower.

For some reason, Charley liked to keep the shower curtain open when she showered, which of course sprayed water all over the floor and countertops, and Savarna said, to put it mildly, "was distracting." Charley said she felt closed in and claustrophobic if the curtain was closed all the way. They eventually compromised and had it halfway open or shut, depending on one's point of view.

Luscious literally came between them at night. She'd always slept with Savarna and been her built-in hot water bottle. Her cat sleeping on her feet, belly, or against her back was commonplace and comforting, but to Charley, Luscious made it so she couldn't snuggle up to her love and at times could barely move because she didn't want to disturb the feline queen. Charley liked cats, but at times Luscious was a little too much.

"Here, Luscious," Charley said, taking the cat off her lap at the dining room table. "Go sit with Savarna." Luscious did just that. They were having a late evening meal together and enjoying the few moments they had when one of them wasn't rushing off to work or family. Charley's mother had already been by a few days earlier, unannounced, to bring them a house-warming gift. She'd heard about the change from her daughter and decided to bring them a few beautiful glass vases filled with roses and sunflowers. Savarna had been taken aback and somewhat embarrassed, but Charley had taken it in stride and appreciated her mother's thoughtfulness. She'd then proceeded to take the couple out for drinks and thrown in a few hints about kids, biological clocks, and grandchildren.

Charley finished the last bite of the Chinese dish she'd made with broccoli and black bean sauce and asked Savarna if she liked it.

"Unbelievable." Savarna sat back and wiped her mouth with one of their good napkins. "That is the best Chinese I've ever had. Where'd you get that recipe?"

"My mother, believe it or not. She had a friend from Shanghai when she lived in Paris, and they traded culinary secrets for years. Nobody believes me when I tell them my French mother cooks the best Chinese."

"It does sound a little odd, but the results are fantastic."

They cleared the plates then each grabbed a book and sat on the sofa. Luscious jumped onto Savarna's lap.

"What are you reading these days?" Savarna asked, craning her neck to read the title of the book Charley had in her hands.

"Just something light, for fun."

"What is it?"

"Nothing really."

Savarna kept trying to see the title, but Charley turned it away and then put it facedown beside her so the cover was hidden. She picked up another large book from the coffee table that was a photographic collection and started leafing through the pages. Savarna stopped trying to pretend she was reading her historical novel about Jewish chicken farmers in 1920s Northern California and turned and stared at Charley. "Don't be childish. What is it?"

"My mom loaned it to me," she said. "I'm not trying to say anything or put on any pressure. It's just in case... I want to be as prepared as possible. I didn't have any brothers or sisters like you did growing up, so I want to make sure I know what I'm doing." Charley grabbed the book beside her and held it up for Savarna to see. The title read, *Spiritual Midwifery*. "Mom said she read this cover to cover when she was pregnant with me and wanted to pass it along in case we ever, and I don't mean right now, but ever... sometime in the future... decide to have a baby."

Savarna smiled, went back to reading her book and said, "Whatever."

"Whatever? It's a little more than that, especially knowing what we know."

"We don't know anything, and you just said you were talking about the future, not now."

"Maybe near future?"

Savarna snapped her book shut. "You know that's all rubbish. They're just making up stuff to try to have me get pregnant. I don't know exactly why they're going to such lengths, but for some reason they've deluded themselves into believing I'm the last chance they have before

The Last Conception

they die."

After her parents had told Savarna and Chitra about their "secret society" and her being the last in line, Savarna had been confused and irritated about the whole affair. She kept it from Charley for a few days and then confided in her and spilled the beans about the "big secret." Charley was much less skeptical and had listened as if she was hearing a confession, like some national or religious holiday.

"I admit that it seems way out there, but it doesn't sound as fabricated as you make it out to be. Besides, having children is something we've talked about before. It's not like it's a big surprise that I want to have children."

Charley gently touched Savarna's elbow. Savarna's hand moved over to Charley's knee. "I understand. Just don't pressure me, OK? I've had enough of that already." They leaned into one another, kissed, then sat back and started reading again.

"Oh, yeah, did I tell you that my grandmother is coming here next week?"

"Here, to our house?"

"'Our house.' Has a nice ring to it. No, not here here. At my parents'."

Charley stopped reading. "That's a big deal, isn't it? Didn't you tell me once that she's a nun or something and never left Thruvananana... something?"

"Yeah, it is a big deal." Savarna put her book in her lap, on top of the cat. "She's never been outside of Thiruvananthapuram her entire life. She became a nun about twenty-five years ago, after grandfather died."

"Did she shave her head and sit in a cave?"

"No, she didn't shave her head or live in a cave. I'm not sure what religious thing she's into."

"Does she have any other children?"

"She had three sons. Dad and my uncles Rakish and Jitvananda, but they both died. She had to cremate them both within two years."

"That's awful. I'm sorry."

"Rakish was in a car accident outside Mumbai, and Uncle Jitvananda died from some lung infection."

"Did they have any kids?"

"Yeah, they both had daughters."

"Where do they live?"

"They don't. Radha and Shiva both died in the tsunami, along with their moms. They never found Radha's body."

Luscious stretched and purred as Savarna scratched her behind the ears.

"That's really sad."

Savarna nodded. "Yeah, they were sweet. I met them a few times. Grandmother sent hundreds of photos of them growing up. They were each quite beautiful in their own way."

After a few moments of silence, with nothing but the sound of Luscious's contentment, Charley said, "So, it's true?"

"What?" Savarna half-replied, as she was thinking about her cousins and the last time she'd seen them in 2001.

"You are the last woman in your family who can bare a child."

"I guess so."

Chapter Eleven

They met Savarna's grandmother, Jitana-Ji Sikand, at the Mineta International Airport in San Jose. Her tiny five-foot frame was covered from head to toe in a blue sari. At first glance some could mistake her as Mother Theresa's twin sister, though Jitana-Ji would be the first to exclaim that she was no saint. Her son, Davidia, was the first to greet her, as she shuffled her way through the crowd, after disembarking from the long flight.

"Mom," he bowed with his palms together in front of his chest, which she returned. Then they hugged. The difference in size between mother and son was so great that she almost disappeared when they embraced.

Mira was next. She started to bend down to kiss her mother-in-law's feet, but Jitana-Ji would have none of that and guided her upwards into a loving embrace, as people walked around their family, some annoyed that this little reunion was not moving out of their path.

"Welcome to America, Grandma," Savarna said, in the best Malayalam she could muster. The eldest Sikand looked up and took a slight step backwards. Then she spoke to Mira.

"What did she say?" asked Savarna.

"She said you are taller and more beautiful than the last picture she saw of you and wondered if you had grown."

"Not lately," Savarna said, smiling. Her grandmother approached, reached up and took her granddaughter's face in her hands, as if she was checking to make sure she was real. Then she put her hands on Savarna's heart and gently moved her palms down to Savarna's belly.

Before Savarna could say anything or react, Chitra intervened. "Grandma!"

"My little Chitra!" Jitana-Ji exclaimed. Everyone understood until she began speaking rapidly. "You are such a strong young woman, and you've been through so much," their mother translated. "I prayed for you every day, and I see you and Mr. Nolan are doing well." She turned to Mike, who had been patiently and happily observing his in-laws, and shook his hand.

"You must be very, very tired," Davidia said. "Let's go get your suitcase and get you home and fed."

"No," Jitana-Ji said. "I'm not tired. Traveling is a perfect opportunity to meditate and pray."

Savarna could see that her Grandmother knew loss intimately. Her face was covered with deep wrinkles, and her stooped shoulders seemed to be carrying hundred-pound water pails. Her eyes were the exception. They shone as bright as sparklers on the Fourth of July.

* * * *

There were enough smiles and laughter to fill a stadium that afternoon at the Sikands. Once Jitana-Ji had been rejuvenated with a little mango lassi and naan, she wanted to see and hear about everything. They led her around the house from room to room. Her son and daughter-in-law proudly showed her how all the new appliances, TV's, dishwashers, and washing machines worked. She'd done without such contraptions since becoming a nun over a quarter of a century ago. She looked at photo albums of the girls, some of which she'd seen from pictures they'd sent her by mail, but many that were brand-new. Savarna and Chitra felt like they were watching a prize-winning documentary of their lives unfolding before them, since Grandma was so delighted with each photo. Even ones that seemed much like the previous page sent her to the moon with ohs, ahs, tears, and laughter. After they reached the last page of the photo albums and what seemed like hours, Jitana-Ji said, "Now, I have something to show you."

Grandmother took Savarna and Chitra by the hand and led them to her guest room, which was Chitra's room when she was a child. Davidia and Mira followed closely. The room was sparse and still had the pink

The Last Conception

unicorn Chitra had drawn on the wall over her bed. The girls sat on the single bed while their parents pulled up the large cushioned chair from the corner and shared the edge of the seat. Jitana-Ji pulled out her small brown old-fashioned suitcase from under the bed and took out an iron container about the size of a shoebox. She sat on the bed between her grandchildren with the box in her hands. Their mother and father translated as Jitana-Ji Sikand spoke.

"What I am about to show you is something very few people on earth have seen. We have hid them, protected them, and cared for them for thousands of years. You have to promise that you will never, and I mean never, tell another living soul where these are from." The girls both nodded, but they thought it was just a joke or something their grandmother had made or brought as a gift.

"Our teacher, bless him always." She closed her eyes, opened them, and continued. "Our teacher wore these all of his life. They have been passed down through our family for generations." Savarna rolled her eyes and snickered. Her grandmother looked at her. "This is serious. I brought them to prove to you and your sister that what your father and mother have been telling you is true. You are the last to know and the only one who can bear fruit." Savarna nodded with as straight a face as she could muster.

The iron box did look old, but anything can be made to look old, Savarna thought. *That's how a lot of antique shops made their living, by pretending some of their items were older than they were.*

When her grandmother's weathered hands opened the creaking metal lid, Savarna and Chitra leaned closer to get a better look. Jitana-Ji carefully removed a folded faded brown robe and said, "This was our Master's robe. He wore it for many years." Their grandmother held it gently to her chest. Savarna and Chitra reached over and touched the fabric. It felt soft as felt and very thin. "Hold this carefully." She placed the robe on Chitra's lap, then reached inside the container once again and brought out a small dark-brown hardwood box that fit in the palm of her hand. As she struggled to take off the lid, Davidia leaned forward to help, but she said, "No. I can get it." After another minute of prying and pulling, the lid loosened and was removed to reveal a gold ring.

Jitana-Ji grasped the ring between her forefinger and thumb. Her hand shook slightly as she held the ring in front of her and said, "This was his wedding ring. It never left his hand until the day he passed from this existence we call life." She took Savarna's hand, lifted it up, and put the ring in the palm of her hand. "This is a million times more precious and valuable than the gold from which it was made."

"Grandma," Chitra said softly, as Savarna got as close to the ring as her eyes allowed and still be able to focus. "Thank you for these wonderful gifts, but it doesn't really prove anything."

"They aren't gifts," Jitana-Ji replied quickly. "I'm taking them home when I return. They will be passed on to your parents when I have left this realm and then to you when they have done likewise." Savarna handed the ring back. "No, you keep these for the time being. You can have them checked if you still don't believe me, but…" she sat up as straight as her curved spine could withstand, "you cannot reveal who they belong to and where you got them."

"Who do they belong to?" Savarna asked.

As her parents translated their grandmother's reply, Savarna and her sister skillfully hid their dismay and disbelief. They didn't want to hurt their grandmother's feelings. Savarna could only handle the situation by pretending that it was all a joke or some part of her grandmother's religious beliefs that needed to be assuaged.

As if reading their minds, Mr. Sikand interjected, "You can get them carbon-dated if you still don't believe us."

"That's OK, Dad," Savarna replied. "We don't need to go to all that trouble."

"No, really," he insisted. "We know a woman who works at the Asian Museum. Her name is Dr. Evelyn Liu. She helped us find a location for the South Asian Dance Festival."

"Of course we remember the festival, Dad," Chitra replied. "We go every year. I don't remember any Dr. Liu though."

"Your father's right," Mrs. Sikand said. "Take the robe and ring to Mrs. Liu. She can tell you when they were made. Your grandmother didn't bring these all this way just for show. She wants you to understand your destiny." She stared directly at Savarna and seemed unwilling to look away until her daughter agreed.

"Ok. Sure," she said. "I'll have Dr. Liu take a look at this old stuff."

The Last Conception

Mira translated what Savarna had said to Jitana-Ji.

"It's not just 'old stuff'," her grandmother said adamantly. "It is proof that you are related to our Great Teacher and are the last in line. Do not take this lightly. It is not just a matter of faith. It is your responsibility and the greatest of all honors."

"I'll do my best, Grandma." Savarna said, as she gave her a hug. Her mind was telling her different. *The last thing I'm going to do is walk into some museum and ask them to date these things and look like an idiot.*

Chapter Twelve

Luscious jumped up with a start and started meowing as she ran towards the front door. Charley almost did the same, except for the meowing. Savarna entered, put her purse and keys on the small hallway table, as well as something that looked like a metal shoebox. She picked up the cat and gave Charley a kiss.

"Did your grandmother make it here OK? How is she? What did she have to say?"

Charley had stayed home at Savarna's request. This was the first time Savarna's grandmother had ever been outside of India, let alone to visit them in California. She hadn't told her about Charley yet, though her parents certainly had by now and Savarna didn't want to overwhelm her with new faces and situations.

"She's wonderful, but she's just as out there with all this religious nonsense as my parents," Savarna said, while grabbing some chocolate soymilk out of the refrigerator and pouring herself a glass. Still holding the cat with one hand and her drink in the other, she made her way to the couch and put her feet up on the coffee table. Charley sat down close to her new feminine housemates and petted the cat in her lover's lap.

"Why do you keep calling it all nonsense? What did she say?"

"The same crap as Mom and Dad. 'You're the last in line. this is your destiny.' That kind of malarkey. It's not really about what she said though, as much as what she brought."

"What are you talking about?"

"That." Savarna nodded toward the entrance.

"What is it? Some kind of family gift?"

72

The Last Conception

"You could say that."

"Can I take a peek?" Charley asked, after she'd already risen and headed towards the hallway.

"Be my guest. Bring it over here before you open it, though. You have to be real careful."

Charley brought the box back to the couch, sat down cross-legged next to Savarna and held the old metal container as if it were a baby. "It looks ancient."

"That's what they say."

"Should I open it?"

Savarna nodded.

Charley opened the squeaking lid and looked puzzled. "What on earth?" Then she gently lifted out the robe.

"Grandmother says that is a robe their Master used to wear when he first started teaching."

"Their Master?" Charley asked, as she turned it around and felt the fabric.

"The guy who started their entire religious tradition. The one I'm supposedly related to."

"And what's this?" Charley asked, after seeing the small wooden box, taking it out of the container, and replacing the robe. Charley opened the little container and held up the ring to the light.

"That, my dear, is what you would call the crème de la crème. He reportedly wore that ring for his entire life."

"How did they get these items?" Charley asked.

"She said they have kept them in the family and passed them down from one family to another for a zillion years." Savarna drained the last of her drink and put the glass on a coaster next to her feet.

"It looks authentic to me," Charley said.

"Looks can be deceiving. You know how easily original paintings can be faked. I'm sure this is the same thing."

"Wrong. This is completely different." Charley put the ring back in the container, placed it in the metal box on top of the robe, and closed the lid. "You can have this carbon-dated to see when it was made. Sometimes they can even tell where it comes from."

"That's what Dad said." Savarna headed toward the bathroom and spoke over her shoulder. "He said there's some lady he knows at the Asian Museum called Dr. Liu. He told me to have her check it out."

Charley put the box on the coffee table and followed Savarna down the hall. She stood outside the bathroom door. "That sounds like a good idea. Why don't you do it?"

"I'm not going to go embarrass myself with some lady at a museum and take up her precious time with fake stuff from India," she replied through the door.

"What if it's not fake? What if you are who they say you are?"

Savarna exited the bathroom rolling her eyes and headed toward the bedroom with Charley on her heels. She suddenly turned, making Charley, who was looking down in deep thought, run into her face first.

"Sorry," Charley said. Savarna just laughed, kissed her passionately, and pulled her into the bedroom. Savarna spread her arms wide and fell back on the bed. Charley covered Savarna with kisses up one side of her neck and down the other then said, "I wish you'd take this more seriously."

"Isn't this serious enough?" Savarna replied, as she caressed Charley's lips with her tongue.

"No, I mean this lineage thing and that ring and robe."

Savarna turned her head to the side, sighed, and sat up.

"Drop it. OK? Just drop it. Even if we had that stuff checked out, I promised to never tell anyone how we got them or where they came from." Savarna stood and started undressing for bed. Charley followed suit.

"Of course not. If any of this is real, they don't want to be exposed," Charley said. She put her jewelry on the nightstand and climbed under the covers.

"The only thing I want to expose is you," Savarna smiled, as she snuggled up to Charley.

Later, before drifting off to sleep, Charley asked what else Savarna's grandmother and family had talked about that evening.

"She told us some stuff about Dad when he was a kid." Savarna smiled. "Some of it was hilarious. Grandma said that Dad was always into food, as if we didn't know that already. She said that he would eat anything, just to see how it tasted. He tried flowers, straw, even mud. His favorite though, which Chitra and I couldn't believe, was snails."

"Snails?"

"Yeah, when he was seven years old he'd eat them raw and lick his lips, as if they were a delicacy."

"I knew it, madam. You *do* have French in your family tree!"

They both giggled.

"The other crazy thing was how much he would go sit in the garden by himself when he was a teenager. She said he would squat down in the middle of the vegetables and look like he was in a trance, sometimes for hours."

"That's interesting. Your dad is so social, that doesn't fit my image of him at all."

"I know. I asked him if that was true, and he said he didn't remember."

"Did she tell you how your mom and dad met?"

"Yeah, but they've all told us that a million times."

"I've never heard it."

"Dad was just finishing teachers' college and Mom had just graduated from high school. She was only eighteen when I was conceived."

"Really? That seems so young."

"Anyway, they were both dressed up for their graduations and had run into a shop to get their parents a gift to thank them for all their support. They had each forgotten to get something earlier and were in a rush. He let her go ahead of him in line to pay and saw that she'd picked out the same basket of soaps, oils, and incense that he had, and he made a comment about it. When she told him it was for her parents, he told her his gift was for his as well. She assumed he was graduating from high school, and he thought she was completing college. He asked for her name."

"I thought marriages were arranged most of the time."

"They were, actually still are, but neither of them had taken to anyone their parents had chosen yet. When he asked about the family, he soon found out where she lived. He was like a private detective and discovered who her parents were and figured out a way to make it seem like his parents had selected her as a possible bride."

"How'd he do that?"

"He found out who the matchmaker was that her parents were using and had a friend sneak in his photo and family background to her collection of possible mates for Mira. Then he did the same thing with his family's matchmaker, Mrs. Rishnananda. That way, both sets of parents believed they were the ones who had found the perfect match."

"What a clever one."

"When they were introduced, my mom realized she'd met him before and was thrilled. She said she'd never stopped thinking about him after their first encounter. It was then that she also discovered he was a college graduate and not high school."

"Ah, what a sweet love story."

"You know what's really sweet about it? I think they're just as in love now as they were then. I hope I can say that someday."

Charley rolled to her side, put her hand on Savarna's chest and kissed her on the cheek. "I hope we can too."

* * * *

The days that followed were jam-packed with work and family. No matter how tired she was, Savarna went to her parents' home right after work to see her grandmother. She heard more stories about her father and other relatives, both living and dead. Jitana-Ji told her some things about her husband (Savarna's grandfather, Govinda Sikand) and asked her repeatedly if she'd had the items she'd brought over authenticated yet. Savarna always promised that she would soon, but never got around to it. She'd heard most of the stories before, by phone and letters, but not in person since she'd last visited India. They all sounded familiar, except the one about her grandfather's family emigrating from the north.

Govinda's parents were northerners, Jitana-Ji informed Savarna after dinner one evening. He was not raised in Thiruvananthapuram, as she had been. When they were married, she'd been told that Govinda and his family had always lived in the south, but he confided many years later, in private, that that was not true. When she'd asked him why his family had lied, he told her that it was necessary to keep everything safe. "Safe from what?" she'd wondered, but been too frightened to ask. He didn't tell her until she was pregnant with Davidia. That's when he told

The Last Conception

her what she was now part of. That's when she discovered that she was part of the lineage, and her son would be the next in line.

That story made sense, with everything else she'd been learning, and less of a fairy tale then her grandmother's previous tales.

* * * *

It was a week after Jitana-Ji had arrived with her "special" items when Savarna came home from an evening with her family and discovered another woman with Charley.

"Savarna! Good, you're home." She kissed her and led her by the hand to the living room. "This is Dr. Liu."

"Very pleased to meet you, Ms. Sikand," Dr. Liu said, rising from the couch. She shook Savarna's hand. It took a moment for Savarna to understand what was happening.

"Do I know you?" Savarna exclaimed.

"This is Dr. Liu," Charley explained. "From the Museum of Asian History."

"Please, call me Evelyn."

"The Dr. Liu my father was talking about?"

"One and the same," Charley replied.

"OK, Charley. What have you been up too?"

"Nothing that you were ever going to do. Sit down."

They sat on the couch, with Dr. Liu seated on the opposite loveseat and the metal box dead center in the middle of the coffee table.

"Do you understand the significance of these items?" asked Ms. Liu, almost jumping off the couch with excitement, as she nodded towards the table.

Savarna turned to Charley. "I said I would get around to this. Who do you think—"

"You were never going to do it and you know it. What's the harm? Are you afraid of the truth?"

"You have no right to go behind my back and—"

"I didn't go behind your back. You promised your grandmother that you'd make sure to get these checked, and since you're so scared of the facts I knew I'd have to do it myself."

"I'm not scared, but—"

"Just listen for once. Please, listen." She nodded towards Dr. Liu.

"It was my pleasure to have these carbon-dated." She picked up the metal container then placed it back on the table. "When Charley showed them to me, my first reaction would have been to dismiss them as fakes, but when she said your father, Mr. Sikand, had referred her, I went ahead. I figured it wouldn't take too much of our time, and there was nothing to lose." Dr. Liu's eyes were almost popping out of her head. "When I got a call from my assistant two days later saying he didn't care where I was or what I was doing but I had to get to the museum right away, I still had no idea how significant these were going to be."

Dr. Liu reached forward and picked up the metal container as if it were a newborn baby and opened the lid. "This robe," she said, as though she were speaking about the love of her life, "is the exact design, material, and age of the dates Charley gave us. And the ring is even older. They are amazingly well preserved and quite authentic, to say the least."

Savarna was shocked.

"You know what this means?!" Charley exclaimed, as she faced Savarna, who subtly nodded affirmation. "It means it's all true. Your parents... your grandmother..."

"What's all true?" Dr. Liu asked.

"Nothing," Charley replied, after a stern stare from Savarna. "Just— just that they are as old as we thought."

"Ms. Sikand. Where did you obtain these precious relics? We would like to get the owner's permission to display them at the museum."

"I can't tell you that."

"But we must have permission before we put them on public..."

"They are not for display. We have to return them to their owner, who we promised would remain confidential."

"Are you absolutely sure?" Dr. Liu pleaded, nervously adjusting the wire-rimmed glasses on her nose, as her right leg shook slightly side to side. "These treasures of Indian history should be available for all to see. I can assure you that we would take the utmost precautions to ensure their safety and integrity."

"It is not up to us. This is a private matter," Savarna replied.

Dr. Liu looked down at the box, her leg still shaking. "Well, at least

The Last Conception

use this, OK?" She reached over the side of the couch and lifted up a stainless steel container. "Put that metal box inside this and keep it sealed. She picked up the ancient iron box, placed it in the new steel container, and slid a lever in the front that made a quiet click. "This is an airtight, vacuum-sealed preservation device that will keep the box, robe, and ring better preserved than ever." She placed everything back on the coffee table.

"Thank you so much, Dr. Liu," Charley said, as she escorted her to the door. "We greatly appreciate your time and expertise."

"It's really a shame that you won't... please let me know if you change your mind or have any questions."

"We will."

As they shook hands, Dr. Liu leaned forward and whispered, "Call me. Please call me."

"Ah, I don't...."

"Promise?"

"Yes, yes. I will."

Charley closed the door after Dr. Liu and returned to the couch, where Savarna was still sitting and staring at the stainless steel box on the coffee table.

"It could belong to someone else," Savarna said out loud.

"It could."

"This can't be happening, is it?"

"I think it is."

"All of those stories, all that baloney about lineage and last in line."

"Yeah, all of that."

"If it's true..."

"And you are who they say you are."

"I wonder."

"What?"

"I always thought their pilgrimages were silly. I know who their teacher is, most people in the world do, but I never felt connected one way or the other. Now, with all this... who knows?"

"Your family knows. You've got to tell them what we've discovered."

"We discovered? More like you."

"You know what I mean."

Savarna leaned forward, picked up the box and held it on her lap. She placed her hand on top. "I'll have to show grandmother how this contraption works."

"That shouldn't be hard."

"What do I do now?" Savarna looked pleadingly at Charley. "What the hell am I supposed to do?"

Chapter Thirteen

Who am I to have a baby? What gives me the right, just because I can? What about all the other women struggling to get pregnant or having miscarriages? There are so many children starving, dying, and suffering in this world. Why add one more mouth to feed? There are lots of kids without homes already. And this whole lineage thing... what's that all about? Even if it's true, and I still have my doubts, should I really go through with this just to please a bunch of religious fanatics who are under the illusion that I'm their last hope to carry on the "bloodline"?

It's all so weird. Part of me has always wanted to have children, but I was never that attached to it being biological. Of course, Charley is totally into the whole thing. I still can't believe she went behind my back to have Grandma's things checked out, but I'm sort of glad she did. It makes making a decision a little easier. As long as it was all ambiguous and hypothetical I didn't have to decide. At least in my mind I didn't. Now, it seems as if destiny has sort of come home in spite of my efforts to avoid it. I hate that word—destiny. It is so loaded and presumptuous. Who knows or decides what is or isn't someone's destiny? People's choices are always influenced by their personal experiences, desires, and belief systems, whether they're conscious or unconscious. I'm just like everyone else. I'm not any wiser or saner about making decisions than the next person, even though I have to make them all the time. Sometimes I get caught in my own hype about how intelligent or smart I am and think I'm the only one that should decide and that I know best. How do I know what's best?

Even if I only did it for my family. Perhaps that is as good a reason as any—to make them happy. And what if it helps their religious group to continue believing in some magical thread or bond with the past in order to shape their future? What's wrong with that? Nothing, I guess. Honestly or as honest as I can be with myself, I think I've always wanted to experience what it's like to carry another life inside of me and give it birth and then nurture it as it grows. It's sort of like preparing the environment for an embryo, having it inseminated, and watching it develop. There is nothing more miraculous that I've ever heard of or witnessed.

And what about Charley? I always told her I'd consider it because it's something she's always wanted to do, but really, I'd do it for me as much as her. And who could ask for a better co-parent? She's got the total mothering vibes and always has. I'm sure we'd have some conflict along the way, but who doesn't? It seems like I've asked myself a zillion times whether I'm good enough to be a mother. I've seen a lot of messed-up kids and families, and no matter how healthy they started out or what their intentions were, they still don't always work out. I mean, you know, things happen. Bad things happen, things beyond our control. We can't control *everything in the lab, no matter how many precautions we take, and we sure as hell can't control everything that happens in life. What if I totally screwed up our kid and didn't even know I was doing it? Ahhhhhh!!! I've got so many questions, and there aren't any clear answers.*

Thousands of women have been doing this for thousands of years. Somehow they've gotten through it and done a damn good job. Maybe that's where all that leap-of-faith mentality comes in. You just have to take the plunge, take a step, reach out, or in my case, do a little mixing and make a deposit.

* * * *

The front door opened and closed with a dull thud. "I'm home," Charley called out.

I guess this is as good a time as any, Savarna told herself, as she closed the journal and locked it away.

"Jenean drives me crazy sometimes," Charley exclaimed, when Savarna walked into the living room.

"Jenean?"

"Jenean, remember?" She leaned her large canvas bags of matting against the couch, which Savarna knew she'd forget about until the next morning. "She's the manager of that little studio in Sausalito." Savarna was still puzzled. "The lady who bought my collection of pastels last fall and then tried to get me to buy back the ones that didn't sell."

"Oh yeah. *That* lady. What happened now?"

Charley made her way to the kitchen and pulled out a quart of grape juice and drank straight from the bottle. Another unconscious etiquette faux pas, which bugged Savarna to no end and one she had been struggling to let slide.

"She called me at the studio and raved and raved about my work and then asked if I'd be interested in selling her any more on consignment." Charley put the juice back in the fridge and wiped her mouth with the dishtowel.

"And that's a problem?"

"Here's the kicker. She said, and I quote, 'Would you make a batch of the same ones you did last time?'" Charley threw the towel on the counter, as if she were trying to throw the memory away.

"That's insensitive, to say the least. You aren't a machine that prints out paintings. You're an artist. How has she stayed in business with that kind of attitude?"

Charley made her way to the couch and kissed Savarna lightly on the cheek as she passed by. She sat down hard and crossed her arms. "I think she's one of those rich biddies who doesn't really care about artists or their work, and just buys stuff as cheap as she can that she knows tourists will pop some cash for when they meander through her 'studio'."

"So." Savarna went over and sat beside her. "Why is this upsetting you so much? You don't have to sell her anything. Your work is at some of the best galleries in the area."

"Exactly, and it's taken me a long time to have my work accepted and appreciated, let alone sold. There are so many creative people struggling morning, noon, and night to produce beautiful, meaningful, or intriguing works of art, and a lot of them don't have any choice but to deal with people like her and compromise everything they do in order to survive."

"Do you want me to picket her shop?" Savarna asked. "I will." She saw Charley smile. "I'll get some friends and some signs. They'll say, 'Cheapskate owner. Doesn't know good art from a bag of chips. Shop here at your artistic peril. The Devil checks here daily for lost souls!'"

Charley burst out laughing. "A bag of chips? The Devil and lost souls? I think that's a little much."

"You think?"

"Thanks for the support, but I think I'll pass on your revolutionary smear tactics. You're right, it's not worth the fight." She pushed off her sandals with her toes and crossed her legs. "How was your day? What's going on?"

"Actually, I've been thinking a lot about you." Savarna smiled and looked down at the coffee table. She started tapping her thigh with the tips of her finger. "Well, to put it more accurately, about us."

"Is something wrong?" Charley turned, looking alarmed.

"No, no. It's all good."

"Well?"

I've been thinking, if you're into it… that we—"

"Have a baby!" Charley almost flew off the couch, then sat back down in a state of semi-frantic control.

"Yeah," Savarna stuttered. "How did you know?"

"I just knew. I just knew. The sheepish look on your face said it all." Charley couldn't stop grinning.

"Well, what do you think?"

"I think it is one of the best things I've ever heard in my entire life." She took Savarna in her arms. "And you are the only person I've ever wanted to have children with."

"What about getting pregnant?"

"What about it?"

"I mean, are you OK with me carrying the child?"

"Absolutely, especially considering the fact that you could be, you know, the last one and all."

"And if I wasn't or am not?"

"I'd still say it should be you. Maybe I'll be the breeder next time."

"Next time?" Savarna stiffened.

"I said maybe, not for sure. I'm really at peace with it either way."

"Are you sure about this?"

"Savarna, you're asking *me* if I'm sure? Where have you been the last two plus years we've been seeing each other? The real question is are *you* sure?"

"I'm as ready as I'll ever be, and with you by my side, I know it will be wonderful."

By the time Savarna and Charley went to sleep that night, their bed sheets were drenched from their expressions of love.

Chapter Fourteen

"Remember Rachael and Vanna?" Charley asked Savarna, as they were turning over the mulch in the community garden for the homeless on a sunny Saturday afternoon and preparing the soil to plant cherry tomatoes, squash, and cucumbers.

"Rachael? Yeah. We met her and her two-year-old son, I think it was Patrick, at that potluck for Jamie and Julia's tenth anniversary in Berkeley somewhere. Last year I think."

Charley took another shovel of compost from the wheelbarrow and threw it into one of the three-by-nine-foot boxes, with chicken wire on the bottom, that they and other members of the nonprofit group had made to prevent the pesky gophers from eating everything they planted.

"I saw her and her partner Vanna at my show in Oakland yesterday."

"Did she like the show?" Savarna asked, then let out a grunt as she lifted a particularly heavy shovel full of dirt, worms, and decayed food scraps into the mix. Charley's latest collection of original pastels had been showing on the walls of the Oakland Art Academy for over a month. Charley stopped by off and on to meet with the director and see which pieces had sold or had any interest.

"Yeah, they both said they did. They were there to sign up for a class in basic watercolor." She squatted down and removed a few rocks with her gloved hands. "They said that since Patrick was in preschool now, they had an afternoon off at the same time and wanted to do something fun together."

"Good for them." Savarna lifted a shovel full of dirt and as she

The Last Conception

turned toward the box some of the dirt fell on Charley's shoes.

"Hey! I don't need any compost," she laughed.

"Sorry." Savarna grabbed a rake to even out her area.

"Anyway, we got to talking and it turns out that Patrick was conceived through artificial insemination. Rachael is the one who conceived and carried him. She gave me all the details, down to the last drop."

Savarna stopped raking and moved closer to Charley. "You think I don't already know how to do it? What on earth do I do every day?"

"But I thought that was different. You help women that can't get pregnant with all kinds of procedures and equipment. As far as we know you shouldn't have any problem in that area."

"It's not that different. You could have asked me."

"I know, but I was afraid you'd get all technical on me, and I just wanted the basics." Charley grabbed the rake from Savarna and started raking her area.

"Listen, there's nothing that technical about it," Savarna said. She looked at the artistic design Charley was making with the rake as she evened out the rest of the soil in the container. "You keep track of your cycle, know when you're most fertile, and then insert some semen into your vagina and let the sperm swim upstream and do their thing."

"I know. That's what she told me, but…" Charley stopped raking and admired the mountain-and-cloud design she'd created. "Who are you going to have donate the sperm?"

"I've been thinking about that longer than I realized I had. There are sperm banks, but I don't want it to be from some stranger. I've been thinking of asking Johnny if he'd lend a hand."

"Lend a hand? That was bad."

"I've never pretended to be a comedian."

One of the organization's clients came by, and without looking, dropped a tray of young vegetable plants right in the middle of Charley's dirt design. He moved on with another tray to the next group down the line.

"I guess that was like a Tibetan pebble design," Charlie smiled. "Here one minute and gone the next."

"Johnny has sort of offered to help in the past."

"For real?"

"Well, not totally. It was always in jest, but I think he would take it seriously or at least think about it."

They each bent down, put the plant tray between them and started placing the plants in rows.

"Johnny's cool," Charley said, as her spade sank into the fertile soil. "I couldn't think of anyone better. He'd have to understand that we don't expect him to be involved as a parent though, right?"

"Of course. I don't think he'd have the time even if he wanted to."

"Are you sure he wouldn't get hung up on it somehow and think it was 'his' or something, just because he makes a little donation?"

"I doubt it," Savarna said. Her hands gently cupped the roots of a tomato seedling and she placed it in the last hole she'd dug. "If he agrees to this I'll make sure we all understand what is and isn't expected."

"He seems healthy and is very kind."

"He is one of the nicest guys I know and very responsible. I'll make sure he has a physical though and everything is checked out first, and I mean everything, including genetic testing. I'm sure he'd want that too."

"You mean if he agrees."

"Yes, of course. If he agrees."

"And if not?"

"If you haven't noticed, there are a few more of the male species walking around who are churning out trillions of sperm on a daily basis."

"I heard some rumor about that. I guess the odds are in our favor."

* * * *

"It's time. Can you come over right away?"

"No problem. I am at your service."

"It's not a 'service.' It's a gift."

"Ah, thank you. That sounds much more civilized."

"It's our pleasure to provide such an inspiring opportunity for you to give."

"The pleasure is all mine."

"So, can you come?"

"Coming is not an issue, but coming at the right time is."

"Ha ha."

The Last Conception

"Yes. I'll be there in thirty minutes. Yvonne is at her grandmother's today, so it's perfect timing."

"We'll greet you with two cups in hand. One with tea and the other... well, you know."

"I know indeed and will enjoy them both. See you soon."

"Thank you, Johnny. You know this means the world to us."

Savarna hung up the phone and nodded to Charley, who was turning almost pink from excitement.

* * * *

Savarna had spoken with Johnny about their desire to get pregnant and asked if he would be open to helping. He'd joked about it in the past, but she'd never taken it seriously. It turned out that he was delighted to have been chosen, after he'd recovered from the shock of hearing about their decision. She hadn't told him anything about her grandmother and everything surrounding the lineage, but he had no reason to ask about such things. They'd both talked for years about whether to have children or not, so he wasn't surprised when it appeared that she was ready to make the big leap.

He'd been a little leery with the speed with which she and Charley were moving, since Charley had just recently moved in with Savarna and had said so. Savarna assured him that even though their living arrangements were new, that they knew each other well and had been seeing one another for over two years. The other concern he'd brought up was how Savarna's parents would react to having a black grandchild. Savarna had thought about this before and told Johnny that she didn't believe it would be an issue. She figured since she was brown, a child that was a mixture of both of their genes would be difficult to pigeon-hole or differentiate and that her parents would be so thrilled to have the next generation born (and all that implied), that they wouldn't give it much attention anyway.

The only prerequisites they'd made sure Johnny understood and agreed with were that he was not to let anyone at work know what they were doing or how he was involved and that he would not be expected to raise the child in any fashion, unless he wished to be an extended family member who occasionally lent a hand. They also all agreed that when the child was old enough and wished to know who the biological father was, they would tell him or her at that time how Johnny was involved and why. The reason for the secrecy at work was because they would all expect her to use their laboratory to get pregnant and might have some judgments about the way she was going about it.

"Here you go." Savarna said, when they welcomed Johnny a short time later. "Fill this to the brim, OK?" She handed him a half-gallon glass milk jar.

"This may take longer than I thought," he replied, as he lifted the large container and held it out in front of him in jest.

"Here's the tea we promised," Charley said, offering him a small white cup of Earl Grey.

"This is more like it," he said and handed back the milk jar.

"How are things working out with your niece?" Savarna asked.

"Great. She's a good kid. The hardest thing is keeping track of everything she's doing. You know, driving her here and there. It's constant, but I don't mind."

"I think it's great what you're doing, Johnny," Charley said.

"Thanks. I think it's great too, but I wish it could have been different circumstances. You know, without my sister being all messed up and all."

"It is what it is," Savarna interjected. "And you never know. People can change."

"Maybe," Johnny replied. "Have you told your parents yet about trying to get pregnant?"

"Not yet," said Charley. "It's a complicated scene, but we will soon."

"Well, I already know they're all gung ho about having a grandchild," Johnny replied. "From what Savarna told me, they're itching for her to have a baby and don't care anymore about whether she's hitched or not."

"That's for sure," Charley said. "They're going to flip out, in a good way, when they find out we're trying to get pregnant."

"Well, nothing's going to happen if we just sit here and talk about it." Johnny smiled. "It doesn't work by osmosis."

The Last Conception

As he rose, Savarna went to the stove and pulled out a small glass jar from the pot of boiled water and handed it to him with a paper towel.

"Do you need anything," Charley asked, as Johnny headed for the bathroom. "We've got a collection of erotic stories. Guys like seeing women with women, right?"

"Absolutely." Johnny stopped and turned around. "Reading about it is not the same as seeing it. I don't need anything. I've got a good imagination. All I'll have to do is think about Vicki, and I'm good to go." He turned and entered the bathroom. Charley put on some music, to give him some privacy, while Savarna retrieved the eight-inch pipette they had previously prepared. A short time later, Johnny returned from the bathroom.

"A gift for m'lady," Johnny said. He bowed and handed Savarna the cup with a few ounces of precious semen. "May you use it wisely."

"Indeed, great prince." Savarna bowed in return and held the cup delicately in her palm.

"We must now make haste and depart to yonder realms," Charley informed their guest. "Merci beaucoup. We can never thank you enough, kind stranger."

"Ah, parting is such sweet sorrow dear maiden. Until we meet again."

"Au revoir."

"Thank you, Johnny," Savarna smiled. She handed Charley the cup, gave Johnny a big hug and kissed him on the cheek. "You know how much this means to me."

"I do. I just hope it takes. If not, you know where to find me."

* * * *

As soon as Johnny left, the women retired to the bedroom. Savarna took off her pants and underwear and lay on the bed with a pillow under her hips. Charley took the pipette, withdrew some semen from the cup, then handed it to Savarna, who promptly inserted the tip as far as she could inside her vagina, then forcefully squeezed the bulb at the end.

"How long do you need to stay this way?"

"About an hour should do it."

Charley leaned over and kissed Savarna's stomach near her hipbone and continued kissing and licking Savarna's skin towards her breasts. "This is supposed to help, right?" Charley whispered, as she lifted Savarna's shirt over her head and continued her mouth's journey over her lover's landscape. Savarna nodded, closed her eyes and sighed.

Whatever will be, will be, Savarna reminded herself, as Charley's tongue gently touched her nipple.

* * * *

Savarna called her parents, sister, and grandmother the following week and told them she was trying to get pregnant. It was most difficult to tell her sister.

"I'm so happy for you," Chitra said, but Savarna could hear the sadness in her voice.

"I really wish it was you," Savarna said.

"Me too," Chitra replied. "I mean, both of us."

"I know what you mean."

"Yes, I know you do. Really, I'm thrilled. I hope it works right away. I can't wait to be an aunt."

"Well, don't get all riled up yet, Aunty. We have no idea if or when I'll conceive. You know there are no guarantees."

"Of course, but you're as healthy as can be. I don't think it will take long."

"Who knows."

"Yeah, who knows."

* * * *

The first thing her mother said, after she yelled for Davidia to come to the phone, was, "We don't need to know any details, just let us know as soon as you know."

"Of course, Mom, but slow down a little here. I only said we're trying. We don't know if or when it will take."

"Oh, it will 'take,' as you say," her mother said. "The women in our family are very fertile, well… we were. Just once or twice and there you go. We get pregnant."

Savarna heard her father's muffled laugh, as if he'd put his hand on the phone."

"Oh stop it!" she heard her mother exclaim. "She's not a child."

"You were saying?" Savarna continued.

"Believe me, once your intention is there and you have the means to match it, it's going to happen. I—"

"We," her father interjected.

"Yes, *we*," her mother said, "have no doubt in your ability to conceive."

"We are very happy for you, dear," her father added. "You will be a great mother."

"Thanks, Dad, I hope *we* will be."

"Yes, of course," Davidia said quickly. "I didn't mean to leave out—"

"I know," Savarna replied. "But I really wouldn't be doing this if it wasn't for Charley."

There was a pregnant silence, which was finally broken when her father said, "Then we'll have to thank Charley as well. And please, give her our best. I'm, I mean we, are sure she'll be a great mother… a parent too."

Mira called for Savarna's grandmother, but she was already standing right behind her son and daughter-in-law.

Davidia informed his mother of the news. Jitana-ji's face lit up. She spoke, and Mira translated for Savarna. She says, 'You are a blessing to us all and your child will be the ultimate blessing.'" Savarna heard more words bubbling forth in the background. "And, she thinks it is time for her to return home and await word of the auspicious occasion."

"Not right this minute!" Savarna said.

"No, of course not," her mother replied.

"We want to see her and return the things she brought."

"She said, 'definitely,'" Mira translated once more.

"What did you find out?" Davidia asked.

"Find out about what, Dad?"

"The robe. The ring. Don't tell me you didn't have them checked by Dr. Liu."

"Oh yes. Well, Charley, I mean, yes *I* had them dated. Dr. Liu actually came to our house and told us about them. Haven't you talked to her?"

"No, I was waiting to hear from you. What did she say?"

"Nothing that will be a surprise to you. She said they date back to the exact time and place you and Grandmother have said they do."

"We told you," her mother said.

"Now do you believe us?" her father asked, after he had translated the news about the robe and ring to his mother.

"Honestly, I don't know."

"You don't know?" her mother almost shouted. "What on earth will it take to—"

"I didn't say it wasn't true, Mom. I just said I'm still not sure. This makes it much more likely of course, but who knows?"

"We do," Mrs. Sikand added. "And you do too, if you open your heart to the possibilities and look at the history of The Master. You know it's been written about extensively, with the exception of the small detail that he had a child."

"You're a scientist," her father said. "Isn't this enough corroborating evidence to confirm who you are and the family from which you come?"

"Good try, Dad, but science isn't any more exact than God. It's got to be true if some scientific fact points in that direction, right?"

"I wasn't comparing science to God or any idea of what or who God is or isn't. I'm simply stating the obvious. It's right in front of your eyes."

"Perhaps she doesn't *want* to accept it," her mother said. "I felt pretty overwhelmed when I found out. It's a big responsibility. In fact, I can't think of anything bigger."

"I'm not denying that, Mom. It's definitely a big deal, and there appears to be some evidence that it could be true, but I can't honestly say that it's certain or that it really matters if it's true or not."

"Doesn't matter?" her mother exploded.

"Now, now Mira," she heard her father's soothing voice. "Hold on, Savarna, your grandmother wants to say something." Savarna heard her parents and grandmother speaking rapidly in the background, and then her father came back on the line. "Mom, I mean your grandmother, told us to stop trying to convince you, that you would believe it when and if you were ready. She said part of you knows the truth already, but it's a little pebble that's still hidden under a big stone of doubt."

Chapter Fifteen

After receiving numerous calls from Mrs. Liu in the following weeks, Charley agreed to meet her at the Japanese tearoom inside the gardens at Golden Gate Park.

Charley entered the gardens and make her way along the stone walkway, up and over the small arched wooden bridge, to the tearoom's back entrance. She saw Dr. Liu sitting between the narrow tables. Dr. Liu waved her hand rapidly. Charley glanced around quickly when they sat, as if she were a secret agent and didn't want to be discovered.

"I can't thank you enough for seeing me," Dr. Liu said. "I understand your hesitancy and have great respect for Ms. Sikand's wishes. As I said when we spoke on the phone, I promise that I will not reveal or pass on anything you tell me to another living soul."

"Or a dead one," Charley emphasized, with a nervous grin.

"Or a dead one," Dr. Liu gave a half-hearted laugh. "You know the items you had us analyze are the most authentic I have ever seen."

"That's what I understand."

"They are in amazing condition, which in itself is quite a feat."

"Yes, that was quite astounding, once you told us their age. I would have guessed a few hundred years, but then again I'm not an archeologist or anything."

"You have no idea what this could mean."

"Not completely, no, but I have a pretty good hunch." Charley leaned forward and whispered, "I know I shouldn't tell you this, but I trusted you the moment we met, and if I don't tell someone I think I'll burst." A green and red-winged dragonfly landed on the table between them. Neither woman spoke, as they observed the insect sunning itself and Charley got the nerve to continue. "I'm living with the heir of one of the most famous men in history."

"What?" Dr. Liu leaned forward, shaking her head. "Say that again."

"Savarna is the last in line. Her parents have been insinuating this for years, but she never believed it—not until her grandmother brought that robe and ring from India. Then it all made sense. Now, we're certain that her parents told her the truth. They've insisted that she have a child to carry on the lineage."

"The lineage? Are you telling me what I think you're telling me? This is no laughing matter. I hope you aren't pulling my leg."

Charley leaned even closer and placed her hand on Dr. Liu's. "I swear on my mother's grave and anything that is holy that Savarna is the last and only woman capable of carrying on the hereditary blood line of the one known as The Master."

Dr. Liu leaned back and watched the dragonfly lift straight up like a helicopter and dart away. "But… historically speaking…"

"I know. I know. It's a lie. They changed the story of what happened so they could keep it a secret. Only a few families are in on it. They meet once a year to stay connected and pass on any needed information. They don't trust speaking to one another by phone or email."

"They still meet?!" Dr. Liu leaned forward. "Where? When? Who are they?"

"I have no idea." Charley turned her head and was momentarily blinded by the sun. "Somewhere in Southern India. That's all I know."

"You've got to find out. I've got to verify this."

"What? I have no way of finding out."

"Ms. Sikand would know."

"I can't ask her to do that!" Charley shook her head. "I haven't even told her I was meeting with you."

"Then you've got to tell her. We need to verify this story. I can't just accept it at face value."

"I can't."

"You can. You must. This could change everything."

"That's what I'm afraid of. Can you imagine the chaos that would ensue if this is true and it was ever leaked?"

The Last Conception

"Of course I can. It would be insane. Savarna and her family would be overrun with media, zealots, scientists, and followers of every ilk and persuasion. That's why I promise it will remain a secret."

"I knew I could trust you. Do you really believe it? Am I being stupid?"

"I believe you've heard what you've heard, and the objects you brought us are real. Nothing is impossible, and this rings true, but then again, it could all be some imaginary tale the Sikands have been passing on for generations, as some way to strengthen their faith or make them feel special. It could all be a hoax, but I think not."

Both women sat back, feeling the weight of what they were discussing.

"I'll talk to Savarna. She wants to have this straightened out as much as anybody. Perhaps she can ask her dad or mom about this year's meeting or something and say that she's considering attending since she's, you know, the next in line and all."

"That's fantastic. As soon as you hear anything, you'll let me know?"

Charley nodded.

"In the meantime, I'm going to scour all of the books, studies, and records I can lay my hands on and look for any other clues."

"I've got to get home," Charley said. She abruptly drained the last of her tea and stood.

"Of course," Dr. Liu replied, as she also arose. "Oh yes. One last little thing."

"What's that?"

"If you could get a saliva sample from Ms. Sikand and drop it off for me at the museum, that would be much appreciated. You can just bring a glass she used or a tissue she's discarded." Charley's shoulders rose. She put her head to the side and raised her eyebrows. "DNA. I'll check Ms. Sikand's DNA with members of the group in India, when I find them."

"When you find them? You're going to try to find them?"

"Absolutely, but don't worry. I won't tell them why I'm there or what I'm looking for. I'll just be another western tourist who got lost and happens to ask a few questions along the way."

"I don't know if I'll be able to find out anything, let alone where they are. I'm not even sure how Savarna will react to all this."

"I know." Dr. Liu put her hand reassuringly on Charley's shoulder. "I'm sure she'll understand. There's nothing to fear and everything to gain."

"Like what?"

"Peace of mind."

"I hope you're right."

Chapter Sixteen

"Don't move. It's only been a half hour," Charley instructed Savarna, who was lying on her back, with her knees open, like a frog that had been turned over and couldn't get up. Another month had passed without success, and Johnny had just given them another "donation," as he liked to call it. This was the third in as many days. They'd had Johnny's semen checked again at another clinic. It appeared that he was as potent as they come and ready to go. "Besides, there's something I have to tell you."

"Right now?"

Charley sat on the edge of the bed. "Yes. I've put this off too long, and I momentarily have you at a disadvantage." She looked down at Savarna's knees. "Promise you won't move?"

"I don't make promises I can't keep, but I'll try." She squinted hard at Charley, boring a hole of inquisition through the space between them. "What have you done?"

"It's not what I've done, it's more what I said." Charley turned away. Guilt was coating her skin like leaking oil on the surface of the sea. Savarna started to sit up. "No, stay put. You promised." Charley pushed Savarna back down.

Before Charley could continue, Savarna said, "You talked to Dr. Liu, didn't you?"

"Yes. I… how did you know?"

"I saw the number on the phone bill several times and called to see if there was a mistake. When I found out it was the number for the Asian Museum, it didn't take long to put two and two together."

"I've been dying to tell you, but I was afraid you'd hate me forever."

"I could never hate you. You can sure piss me off sometimes, but hate…"

"How long have you known?"

"For about a week. I was waiting to see if you'd come clean and tell me yourself."

"Well?"

"How could you? I mean, why?"

"Do you realize how big this is? We're not talking about a little fable passed on from one family to another. We're talking about history being turned upside down and you possibly being the center of one of the biggest secrets of all time."

"Even more reason to keep our mouths shut."

"Of all people I'd have thought you would want to validate these claims beyond any reasonable doubt, but you've been the most reluctant."

"Of course part of me wants to, absolutely." Savarna lifted her hips and readjusted the pillow. "But, it's also as scary as hell. How could I ever live up to their expectations or be the woman they envision me to be? I can't. I've never been involved in any religious dogma or group, let alone been seen as the head of some order or group of monks, nuns, priests, ministers, rabbis… whatever they are."

"I don't think they're asking you to do anything or be anything other than who you are. They just want you to birth the next in line."

"So… what did she say when you told her?"

"At first, she looked kind of mystified. Who wouldn't? Then, I swear, I thought she was going to jump up on the table and dance. She said, 'It all fits. That 'there is a strong possibility.'"

"She believed you?"

"I think the information she got from the ring and robe had already moved her way beyond the initial disbelief that you, I should say we, had." There was an uncomfortable silence. Charley put her hand on Savarna's stomach. "I'm really sorry. I shouldn't have done it."

Savarna gazed at Charley's downcast face. "I'm not. I was too scared to do anything. I'm glad you did."

"What about the promise you made to your parents and

grandmother?"

"I kept it," Savarna smiled.

"There's something about Dr. Liu that I totally trust."

Savarna smiled at Charley when she replied. "Yeah, me too. She's not the kind of person who goes around blabbering about things. Not like some people I know." Charley started to object, but realized Savarna was playing with her. "What did she want? Is there anything more we can do to help firm this up?"

"She wanted me to get a sample of your saliva, so she can check the DNA with your family in India. She already kept a piece of thread from the robe."

"That's no problem."

Charley cleared her throat. "She also wants to go to India and meet the people who attend the yearly meeting."

"What?"

"She said she'd do it very carefully and nobody would know who she was or why she was there."

"She's got to be kidding. She'd stand out like a rooster in a wolf's den. Everybody would know who she was and why she was there. Thiruvananthapuram is not like the Bay Area. Everyone is into everyone else's business and she's about as southeast-Asian-looking as you are."

"She said she'd go as a tourist."

Savarna shook her head. "No, she may have the best of intentions, but it would never..." Savarna stopped mid-sentence and cocked her head sideways.

"What?"

"I'll go."

"You'll go? You'll go where?"

"I'll go to India and see for myself. I think it's just about time for their yearly meeting."

"You mean 'we'll go.'"

"No." Savarna cupped Charley's cheeks with her hands. "They wouldn't trust you, and Mom and Dad will not give me the information if they know you're coming."

"But... it's so far away and... we're in this together." A tear rolled down towards Charley's chin.

"We *are* in this together and I will miss you terribly, but you know this is the only way it will work."

Charley nodded.

"Give me my pants, will you?" She turned on her side and pushed herself to a sitting position. "I've laid around long enough."

Charley handed her her underwear and slacks. "If any of those little tadpoles made it far enough upstream, they're dancing the two-step by now."

Chapter Seventeen

A month passed and there was still no baby. They'd tried six times by then and had Johnny double-checked to make sure it wasn't because of his side of the equation that everything wasn't going according to plan. The next step was Savarna being evaluated to see if there was anything mucking up her tubes or reproductive "machinery," as she sometimes said sarcastically, giving her a slight sense of detachment from her own stubborn anatomy. But before those tests could be done, there was the issue of a little sightseeing trip she had to look into.

* * * *

"Thanks, Mom," Savarna said, as her mother handed her a cup of tea. They were sitting in her mother's well-tended garden in the late afternoon. Her father was still at work, and they hadn't said much since retiring to the backyard and taking up their seats under the green sun umbrella.

"I have to tell you something and ask a favor."

"How do they say, 'Shoot'?"

"Well," Savarna grinned at her mother's latest attempt at English slang. "So far, it hasn't worked."

"What hasn't worked?"

Savarna put her hands on her lower abdomen. "This baby-making thing hasn't quite taken off yet."

"Why not? Have you tried?"

"Of course, Mom. I wouldn't expect it to happen by magic."

"Um... how many, you know... how many times have you tried?"

"About six, and it was always at the most fertile time of my cycle."

"You had sex with a man six times!"

"No." Savarna had to laugh at the shocked expression on her mother's face. "Not directly. A good healthy friend of ours made a donation each time."

"A donation?"

"Mom."

"Oh, I see." Mrs. Sikand's light-brown cheeks turned a little red. "Don't make fun of me. I'm not that out of touch. I get it."

"Of course, Mom. You're quite the hipster."

"The hipster?" She looked down at her hips. "They haven't gotten that big, have they?"

"Not your hips, I mean..."

"Hah! Got you!" It was her mother's turn to grin. "I know what 'hipster' means. It's like cool or hot or bad or something, right?"

Savarna just nodded.

"I'll have to get some tests done to make sure I'm not infertile."

"You can't be. It's impossible. You haven't had any disease; you're young and you're healthy."

"It's not impossible, Mom. I need to check just to make sure."

"Well, get it done right away. We'll pay for it if you need to."

"We can pay for it, thanks, but there's something else I need to do first."

"And that is?"

"I want to go to India and meet those people."

"What people?" Her mother fidgeted in her lawn chair.

"You know what people. The ones that meet each year to talk about family lines, the lineage and all that."

"I thought you didn't believe it."

"Well... it could be possible, and since I'm the one trying to get pregnant and supposedly continue this thing, it seems that I should meet the people that are into it."

"The Keepers of the Seed," her mother replied quietly.

"The what?"

"The Keepers of the Seed. That's what we're known as, and you cannot reveal that you know anyone who belongs, not even your father and me."

"Of course not," Savarna said quickly, trying to suppress a smile. "Who came up with the catchy name?"

"Don't make fun of it," her mother said. She lightly slapped Savarna on the knee.

"OK, OK."

"I guess you have the right to go, but you cannot have your friend or anyone else with you."

"You mean Charley?"

Her mother nodded.

"I know that. I already told her it was a trip I had to make on my own."

"Good, then you understand."

"I don't like it, but I understand."

"It just happens that the next gathering is the first of next month. Your grandmother was going to go and let everyone know about the situation here. They called a special meeting. You can meet her and she'll take you. We cannot tell you exactly when or where ahead of time."

"I'll have to arrange to have someone cover for me at work. What about Dad? Will he be OK with this?"

"No problem. I'll talk with him tonight, and by the time we're done he'll think it was his idea." They laughed. "And those tests. First thing, when you get back, OK?"

"Absolutely."

Chapter Eighteen

"The heat! My God. I don't remember it being like this." Savarna exclaimed in the best Malayalam she could. Her grandmother, who met her at the airport in Mumbai, nodded in agreement but seemed to look a little bewildered. "I guess she's used to it," Savarna said to the older woman standing next to Jitana-Ji in a dust-covered brown robe.

"I'm Jasmine. Jasmine Bacharyami. You don't remember me, do you?"

Savarna smiled helplessly.

"That's OK. The last time I saw you, you were about this high." She put her hand out in front of her about four feet off the ground. "I've been a friend of your family it seems like forever. I live in Goa. Jitana-Ji asked if I'd travel with her to pick you up. Let me take your bag." She reached for Savarna's suitcase.

"Thank you, Ms. Bacharyami, but I've got it. It's easy. It has wheels."

"Please, call me Jasmine and don't worry, I know about everything. I'm one of them." Savarna hurried ahead, as the two elders walked slowly and purposefully behind. "There's no rush," Jasmine said, just loud enough for Savarna to hear. "The next train to Thiruvananthapuram isn't for another six hours." Savarna slowed until they all walked even.

"How long is the train ride? About a day?"

"More like a day and a half," Jasmine said. "If we're lucky and nothing happens."

"What could happen?"

"Anything," Jasmine chuckled. "This is India."

The Last Conception

* * * *

Hours later, the three women were squished together on a bench in third-class speeding south. Savarna was sure she would faint from the humidity but needn't have worried. Before she knew it, her head was in her grandmother's lap and she had fallen fast asleep with the rocking of the car.

Everything had happened so fast. Her mother had spoken to her father, who in turn contacted his mother, and before she knew what hit her, she had a round-trip ticket to Mumbai and back. As far as locations or who and when she would meet anyone, it was all kept hush hush. All she knew was that her grandmother would meet her at the airport and take it from there. Before she'd even gotten on the plane in San Francisco she missed Charley, and even more so as she'd flown east across the Atlantic. She knew there was no way in hell they would have let Charley accompany her, but it pained her to be doing this alone. At the clinic, Johnny had agreed to work extra time while she was gone and supervise a temp, who had worked with them in the past and could be completely trusted.

* * * *

"We're there," Jasmine said in her British-accented English, pushing lightly on Savarna and Jitana-Ji's legs as they pulled into the station. Savarna lifted her head from her grandmother's shoulder. That was the third time she'd fallen asleep since they'd left Mumbai the day before. She had wanted to take in the beautiful countryside and get a taste of the ancient landscape, but the jet lag and steady beat of the train forced her heavy eyelids to close, in spite of her best intentions.

"What? We're there?" Savarna yawned and rubbed her eyes.

"That was easy," her grandmother remarked in Malayalam.

"What did she say?"

Jasmine laughed and translated. "She said that was easy. She's amazing. She could be two-hundred-years old and still outwalk, outcook, and outsilence the best of us."

"Yeah, she's a strong cookie, that's for sure," Savarna acknowledged. She stood, stretched and grabbed her suitcase. "But what do you mean 'silence the best of us?'"

Nodding at Jitana-Ji and picking up the small bag the two elders had between them, she replied, "She can go weeks or months without speaking, yet say everything."

"That doesn't make sense."

"It will. You'll see."

"I'm not going to be here that long. I only have a week before I have to get back."

"It's not a matter of time, Savarna," Jasmine said. She stepped off the train and helped Jitana-Ji and Savarna onto the platform. "It's what happens between the past and the future that's important, and your grandmother has a knack for being in that place more often than not."

They were immediately surrounded by a dozen men yelling at them at once. Savarna backed away, but Jasmine stood her ground, scanned the faces of those vying for their business and approached a gentleman who was standing quietly to the side and had simply raised his hand.

"Your name, good sir."

"Bhakti."

"With a name like that, you can surely take us to Bingham Road, can you not?"

Bhakti shook his head side to side, then bowed with a smile. "It would be my honor, Mother."

He led them to his elaborately decorated cycle rickshaw, which had a statue of Krishna on the front and the entire canopy covered with orange and yellow flowers.

"What did you mean by 'a name like that?'" Savarna asked Jasmine, as they were seated.

"Bhakti means devotion and to be of service," Jasmine explained, as they were wheeled through throngs of people in every size, shape, color, and various states of dress or undress.

"This is crazy," Savarna said out loud, her eyes wide open, taking in every sound, sight, smell, and sensation that was invading her senses.

Jasmine translated Savarna's words to Jitana-Ji, who replied, "No, this is life."

Thirty minutes passed before they arrived at No. 10 Bingham Road. Jitana-Ji paid their driver and invited him to join them for some tea. Bhakti bowed, with his hands together in front of his chest, and accepted her invitation. During tea, he showed them a picture of his wife and daughter and told them how his father had also been a driver for the British, back in the forties, and explained to Savarna how many of the streets in southern India had kept their English names. Jasmine told them about the Portuguese in Goa and the thousands of people who converted to Catholicism as a result.

"Are you Catholic?" Savarna asked Jasmine, who translated for Mrs. Sikand, who laughed loudly.

"No, but any path to what some call God is a good path."

"Yes. Yes." Bhakti agreed.

After finishing tea and Bhakti thanking them profusely for their hospitality and saying he had to get back to work, Savarna was shown to her room. It was the same room in which they had tea. She realized that her grandmother lived in a one-room house, with no more than a small kitchen and bathroom in the back. There were mats against the wall, which she assumed would be her bed, and other than a couch and coffee table, an old storage bag in the corner. Thank goodness there was also a ceiling fan. It didn't seem to make much difference, but it did send an occasional puff of air, which ruffled the static, stale heat to disperse ever so slightly and provide brief moments of relief.

"So," Savarna said, after stowing her suitcase, "when is the meeting? When do I get to meet this 'secret' group of fanatics?"

"They aren't fanatics," Jasmine retorted. "And please, keep your voice down."

Savarna looked around the room and out the windows and open door. "What are you shushing me for? There's nobody around."

"There's always someone around," Jasmine replied. "In India, everything has eyes, and tongues wag faster than water."

"OK. OK," Savarna said quietly, in spite of her mind telling her Jasmine was totally paranoid. "When do I get to meet these people?"

Jasmine translated for Mrs. Sikand, who approached Savarna, put her hand on her shoulder and said, "We are 'those people' and you'll meet the others soon enough."

Two days later, in the early evening when the temperature was almost bearable, Jitana-Ji and Jasmine took Savarna out shopping. They visited one small stall after another, looking for "just the right curry,"

Jasmine insisted. Every time they stopped at a vendor with a colorful display of green, red, orange, and yellow curries, Jasmine and Mrs. Sikand would stick the tip of their finger on the top to taste the flavor. After winding their way through what seemed to Savarna like an endless, senseless maze and stopping at what she was sure were at least twenty-five shops, Jasmine exclaimed, "It's got to be here somewhere."

"What on earth is wrong with the ones we've been too?" Savarna sighed.

"They're OK, but we want to make you a special southern dish that you'll never forget and it requires just the right combination of curries. For some reason, all the usual places don't have any today, and we don't want to settle for anything less than the best."

"That's all right with me." Savarna looked like she was wilting. The sari they had loaned her was clinging to her body like a wet towel, and strands of her hair were stuck to her forehead and neck.

"You look exhausted," Jasmine said, as she looked at Mrs. Sikand and nodded towards their guest. Jitana-Ji shook her head in acknowledgment and gently brushed some hair out of Savarna's face, as she said something in Malayalam to Jasmine.

"Ah, that's a good idea," Jasmine said.

"What?" Savarna said, standing up straight and trying to muster some energy to not appear like a weak westerner to the two elders doting upon her.

"A friend of your mother's lives close by. We'll stop for a visit, get some tea, and let you refresh yourself."

"No, really," Savarna insisted. "I'm fine. I don't want to impose on anyone."

"Come on," Jasmine said, grabbing Savarna by the sleeve. "It's no imposition. We haven't seen her or her family in months, and she'd be pleased as punch to see you again."

Mrs. Sikand had already turned and walked around the next corner.

"What's her name?" Savarna exclaimed when they caught up with Jitana-Ji.

"Mrs. Um… Mrs. Rishikeshama," Jasmine replied. Jitana-Ji turned her head and nodded in agreement.

They turned another corner and stood in front of a two-story apartment complex that looked like it had been built in the sixties and resembled dozens of other structures that lined the street. There was no address or names on the front of the building.

"Here we are," Jasmine said. They went inside and came upon a center courtyard. Savarna looked up and saw clothes lines strung from one side to the other with loincloths, saris, underwear, socks, slacks, dress shirts, and white t-shirts, as well as large green plants in colorfully painted pots in every corner. They made their way to the second floor, up stairs that creaked and moaned like a sad ghost and knocked on an open door to one of the apartments.

"Hello!" Jasmine yelled.

"Hello, Jasmine and Mrs. Sikand! What a wonderful surprise!" a woman replied, as she hurried towards them from the kitchen. "I was just making some tea for my family. Please, have a seat."

As they entered, Savarna saw more people to her left in the small living room.

"We'd love to," Jasmine said. "This is Jitana-Ji's granddaughter, Savarna. She's visiting all the way from California in America. We were out shopping and she's a little tired. Not used to the heat, you know."

"I'll be," Mrs. Rishikeshama exclaimed, as she bent forward and bowed. "I haven't seen you since you were a little girl. I remember you and your sister getting into everything, including my late husband's shoes one day. They were at least three times your size, and you and Chitra kept tripping over yourselves trying to escape before we saw you."

"I'm sorry," Savarna said shyly, "I don't remember."

"This is my family." Mrs. Rishikeshama turned and made the introductions. "The tall man here in the business suit is my oldest son, Narthak. He's a supervisor at a big-shot service center. He's got to get back to work soon."

Narthak stood, bowed, and extended his smooth large hand to Savarna. They shook firmly. "This is indeed a great honor. I've known your grandmother since I was a little boy and heard about you often."

"The pleasure is mine," Savarna replied.

"That old man at the end of the couch is my brother Rajev, and the woman at his side is his wife Mitra."

The couple looked like spitting images of pictures Savarna had seen of Mr. and Mrs. Gandhi in the 1940s. They rose and bowed deeply. They said something in a language that didn't sound at all like Malayalam and bowed again.

"They're from the north," Mrs. Rishikeshama explained. "They don't speak English or Malayalam. They said it is an honor and a privilege to make your acquaintance. They are good friends of your parents."

They spoke again, bowed for a third time, and sat down. As Savarna returned the bow, her host translated. "They wish for your happiness and ask you to give their kind regards to your parents."

Savarna nodded. "I will. Thank you."

A middle-aged woman remained in the center of the sagging brown couch with her eyes fixed on every move Savarna made.

"And this sweet lady is my half-sister, Aja, who is visiting us from Delhi."

Aja started to kneel, but saw her sister shaking her head. She stood and bowed instead. "I have been waiting… I mean… it is a pleasure to meet you Savarna. Your family and ours have always been close, but I never had the privilege of meeting you in person, since I was married and moved soon after your parents left for the States."

"You look familiar," Savarna replied. "I think I've seen you in some of our family photo albums, or grandmother told me about you."

Jitana-Ji simply nodded and smiled, as she had been doing throughout the introductions, not understanding most of the English, but she picked up on the unspoken energy that was vibrating between those present.

"Sit down. Sit down. Please," Mrs. Rishikeshama insisted. "Let me get the tea. It's probably over-steeped by now."

As their host quickly returned to the kitchen, Savarna and Jasmine gratefully sat and filled up the remaining space on the couch and Jitana-Ji lowered herself to sit cross-legged on a small carpet next to the only other piece of furniture in the room, a small, round coffee table.

Over scrumptious trays of cashew sweets called kaju katli and bountiful cups of tea, Savarna was asked repeatedly about her life, her family, her past, and her future. It actually seemed hotter and more exhausting inside, answering all their questions, then it had been out on the streets looking for curry, but something about the gathering gave her more energy than she'd expected. Mrs. Rishikeshama and her relatives seemed to have no sense of time or a care in the world. It was as if Savarna was all that mattered. She couldn't quite put her finger on it. Not one to seek the limelight, she kept trying to divert the conversation to other things, but it always ended up back on her.

When they said they had worn out their welcome and must get home, it was almost pitch black outside. Savarna was relieved when Jasmine hailed a pedal cab for their return. Even though the heat had died down, along with the sun, she felt a wave of expectation that made her want to go somewhere to lie down and escape.

Three days later, Savarna was almost beside herself with worry. Neither Jasmine nor her grandmother had said another word about meeting the Keepers of the Seed and she was flying back to the States the next morning. She had given up on asking when the gathering was going to happen because she was always told it would be the next day or "sometime soon." Well, the next day wasn't hacking it anymore, and she was not about to have dropped everything and come all the way to southern India for a week to simply pack her bags and go back home to tell her family and Charley that she'd had a nice time with her grandmother, but never had a chance to meet the people who were so insistent on her having a child and carrying on the lineage of the "great teacher."

"Grandmother. Jasmine. This is it," Savarna exclaimed at dinner, on the last night of her stay. "I don't care if we have to stay up all night. I'm not going to leave without meeting the people I came to see, no offense to you. It has been a wonderful stay and your hospitality has been beyond what I could ever expect, but this trip was for a specific purpose, and you know what that was."

Mrs. Sikand listened, while Jasmine translated. They both laughed.

"I don't see what's so funny." Savarna frowned.

"Of course not," Jasmine said, patting Savarna's knee. They were sitting on the floor around the small table in the living room for their evening meal.

"Really," Savarna said. "What's going on? Where are these people?"

"They…" Jasmine started to explain.

"They don't really exist, do they?" Savarna interrupted. "I knew it." Savarna stood up and went to the window. "This has all been a big hoax, hasn't it? There is no 'secret' group. There is no lineage or special bloodline that has been passed from one generation to another."

"Oh, there is," Jasmine replied calmly. "There is indeed." Savarna was completely confused. "Come. Sit back down." Jasmine nodded to Savarna's spot at the table. Savarna walked back slowly, keeping her eye on her grandmother and her friend, who looked at one another conspiratorially, as Savarna knelt back on the carpet. Mrs. Sikand moved her head up and down, indicating for Jasmine to speak.

"You already met them."

"I met them?" Savarna racked her brain to recall any possible meeting. "We haven't been to any special place or religious center. The only people we've met are a bunch of your friends and relatives. It seems like you know a zillion people. Everywhere we go, someone says hello to Jitana-Ji or bows as if they recognize her, but we haven't been to a—" Savarna stopped short. It hit her like the heat had when she stepped off the plane. "Wait… you mean…" Her hosts both nodded, having seen the light of understanding suddenly sparkle from Savarna's eyes. "Mrs. Rishikeshama… her relatives… Narthak, Aja, Rajev and his wife Mitra… that was them?"

"Yes," Jasmine replied with a sly grin, "but other than her brother Rajev, that wasn't her family. There were only three other members of the group that couldn't make it, and believe me, they've already heard all about it."

"I feel like such a fool. I couldn't understand why everyone was asking me so many questions and seemed so excited. It didn't make sense. Something seemed odd, but I forgot all about it." After a few minutes of silence and reflection, Savarna said, "Could you please give me Mrs. Rishikeshama's address, so I can at least write them and thank them for their hospitality and coming all that way to meet me?"

Jitana-Ji shook her head after Jasmine told her what Savarna had requested. "No, we can't do that," Jasmine explained. "Those weren't their real names and a friend of a friend was letting them use that apartment just for the day, so they could meet you. They all left days ago."

"But if I'd only known. I could have gotten to know more about them. I could have told them more about me, what I'm doing, what our plans are. You know, it could have been more meaningful."

"Don't worry, Savarna," Jasmine said. "It was meaningful. They were ecstatic with your presence and hearing you speak. They already know about all your plans and current attempts to conceive. Nothing could have brought them more joy."

"But it's not working."

"What do you mean?" Jasmine asked. Jitana-Ji saw the worried look suddenly appear on her friend's face.

"I haven't been able to get pregnant. We've tried six times and nothing has happened. I spoke with Mom just before coming and we're having tests done as soon as I return."

Jasmine told Mrs. Sikand what Savarna had just said, and it was the first time Savarna had ever seen her grandmother look worried or confused. After a moment's pause, Jitana-Ji looked directly at Savarna and spoke with fire in her eyes.

"She says," Jasmine explained, "that you WILL get pregnant. Whatever has happened up to this point does not matter and does not determine your course. It only takes one time and that will occur when it is most auspicious to do so. This is something beyond your control. Don't give up. Trust that it will happen."

"I wish it was that easy. I don't have that kind of faith or belief, Grandma, but I'll do my best."

"It has nothing to do with faith," Jasmine translated Mrs. Sikand's reply. "It is simply a reality waiting to happen. His bloodline must continue."

"I don't know about that, Grandma. Like I said, I'll do my best."

Chapter Nineteen

"It never felt so good," Savarna told herself, as she was lying in Charley's arms, telling her about her trip—who she met and everything that did and didn't happen.

"So, they exist," Charley said, stroking Savarna's cheek. "They are real after all."

"Well, I wouldn't go that far. The people I met definitely knew my grandma and Jasmine, but they could have been anybody."

"Didn't you say one of them looked familiar?"

"Yeah, I'm sure I've seen Aja before, but that doesn't mean anything. She could be an old family friend, or I just saw her in a photo somewhere."

"But you told me once that your family never kept pictures of anyone, other than your sister and you, which always seemed a little odd."

"They said it was to protect our privacy or something like that. We don't even have a photo of Grandmother, so I'm not sure why I recognized Aja."

"It's because she's one of the Keepers of the Seed, sweetie." Charley ran her fingers along a long strand of Savarna's hair that had fallen out of its braid and followed it to her lover's soft stomach.

Savarna slid her hand down on top of Charley's and held it there.

"Maybe or maybe not. Either way, there's going to be some big-time grief if we can't get any of those seeds to take hold and make a bambino."

Charley gently rubbed Savarna's abdomen in small circles.

The Last Conception

"Whatever happens happens. Let's just roll with it, OK?"

"That's easy for you to say. You don't have the pressure of pregnancy pressing on you like a gigantic expectant mother bear ready to slap you senseless if you don't follow through."

Charley took her hand away. "Who wanted to have a baby in the first place? Who was it that agreed that it should be you because of your family? Who was it…"

"I know," Savarna said. She took Charley's hand and placed it back on her tummy. "I know you want it as much as I do. I'm just saying…"

"I get it. I really get it. I can't imagine what it's like—the expectations of so many people riding on this. Just don't forget I'm here every step of the way, and whatever we go through, *we* go through it together."

* * * *

Savarna had just gotten over her jet lag and gone back to work, when Dr. Liu called Charley at home to find out what had happened and get the scoop on how she could meet the family in India and attend one of their secret meetings.

Charley told her exactly what she wanted to hear and what she and Savarna had agreed upon when she'd returned.

"You can give it a shot," Charley said, "but Savarna doubts you'll get anywhere."

"I understand. I understand," Ms. Liu replied. "So, what can you tell me?"

"Savarna said I could give you her grandmother's address, Mrs. Jitana Sikand."

"Yes. Yes."

"She lives in Thiruvananthapuram in southern India at No. 10 Bingham Road."

"No. 10 Bingham Road in Thiruvananthapuram. Can you please spell that?"

"T h i r u v a n a n t h a p u r a m."

"Got it."

"She's the only person we know of that has a connection with the group, and we can't tell you how."

"Do you think she would tell me anything? Does she have material I could use for further verification?"

"I doubt it."

"And she's the only person Savarna met that knows about this group and the lineage?"

"Well, she met some others but didn't know who they were until later and has no idea where they are or what their real names are. And there was a woman named Jasmine, but she's sure that she's long gone."

"Others?"

"Yeah, others, but it was all through Mrs. Sikand. If you're going to have any luck at all, it's going to be through her."

"Thank you, Ms. Burnnell. Thank you so much and thank Savarna. You have no idea—"

"Oh yes, we have an idea. Believe me, we have lots of ideas."

"I'll have to make arrangements right away and clear my schedule. Oh yes, how should I introduce myself to Mrs. Sikand?"

"Savarna said you should tell her that you are a colleague of hers from work and wanted to see the real India on your travels. Tell her that Savarna knows a friend of hers is a friend of her grandmother's. After that, you're on your own."

"I'll have to get a hair sample, but that should be easy."

"Oh yeah, one other thing."

"Yes."

"She doesn't speak English. How's your Malayalam?"

"Well, I don't speak it at all and I doubt she speaks any Chinese."

"Yes," Charley said with a laugh. "I don't think so."

"That's no problem. I'm sure I can find a translator there somewhere. Is there anything else I should know?"

"Yes," Charley said. "Savarna said to not expect much."

"Absolutely. I understand."

* * * *

"Let the testing begin!" Savarna exclaimed, trying to make light of the situation when she and Charley visited a local Sunnyvale clinic. She knew about all of the tests available but had never had them done on herself. She had explained to Charley ahead of time what the first steps would be—some blood tests at different times of her cycle to check the levels of her follicle-stimulating hormone, her luteinizing hormone, and her ovarian reserve, which can help determine her potential to reproduce. They would also check for STDs, since they are a leading cause of infertility, though she was certain that would not be an issue.

Johnny had already had his sperm tested for health, function, and binding and they were all "good to go," as he would say. So, they knew if something was amiss it was taking place because of some quirk or misfire in her system and not his.

After a physical exam by the internist they'd been referred to and instantly connected with, Dr. Jordan Mathias, and three blood tests over the next four weeks, they were given the "good news and bad news."

"The good news," Dr. Mathias explained, "is that so far all the results show that your hormones and reproductive system is doing exactly what it should be doing, and nothing is out of balance. The bad news is that we need to go to the next step, which is—"

"An endometrial biopsy," Savarna said.

"That's right."

"And what does that mean?" Charley asked.

The doctor nodded towards Savarna, knowing she wanted to be the one to explain.

"They take a small part of my uterine lining and check to see if it will develop enough for an embryo to implant itself."

"Do you have to be cut open? Is it painful?" Charley asked.

"No," Dr. Mathias replied. "We insert a catheter through her cervix up into the uterus and remove a small tissue sample. Then we send it to the lab, and they check to see if the cells are accurate for the time of the month they were taken." The doctor turned towards Savarna. "Where are you in your cycle right now?"

"My period should start in the next three to five days, if I'm on schedule."

"She always is," Charley said, "like clockwork."

"That's perfect timing," Dr. Mathias said. "If you have another twenty minutes, I can fit you in and do it right now."

"You can do it here, in the office?" Charley asked.

Dr. Mathias and Savarna both nodded.

"OK, with me," Savarna said. "Better than having to make an additional appointment."

* * * *

Before they knew it, Savarna and Charley were back home. The procedure had caused a little discomfort and tired Savarna out more than she'd expected, but it wasn't as bad as it had sounded to Charley. The results came in a few days later—negative. The cells in Savarna's uterine lining were healthy and perfectly matched for her time of the month.

The next step was more involved and invasive—a laparoscopy. Charley knew right away that this procedure involved cutting small incisions above and below Savarna's naval. They were both more apprehensive this time around. Savarna had never had surgery and was reluctant to have general anesthetic. She asked for and received a local, which worked out just as well and had fewer side effects. Dr. Mathias had explained, more to Charley than Savarna, that the laparoscopy made it possible for her to use a small telescope to peer inside and evaluate the health of the ovaries, fallopian tubes, and uterus. She'd film it and show them the "Academy Award-winning movie" after Savarna had fully recovered.

They saw the doctor the day after the outpatient surgery and were shown the film of the procedure. Dr. Mathias said Savarna's organs looked completely "in tune" and were running "like a well-oiled sports car".

"Actually, she has an electric car and doesn't use oil," Charley piped in.

"Well, you get my meaning. Sorry for the automobile analogy. In more down-to-earth terms, your body appears to be functioning just as Mother Nature intended."

"So, what's the next step?" Charley asked.

"The last thing we can try before IVF," Dr. Mathias replied, "are fertility drugs."

"Drugs?" Charley questioned with a look of concern.

"Yes, drugs," the doctor replied. "You will be monitored closely. We can try several that have been very successful… one at a time." We'll give each one three to four months to see if they work. If not, you know what's next."

Savarna nodded and turned to Charley. "I'm OK using pharmaceuticals. Ones for fertility have been well-tested, and I totally trust Dr. Mathias' opinion and experience."

"If you're OK with it," Charley said. "Let's give it a shot."

"Actually, it's going to be pills at this stage, not shots," Savarna explained. "The shots will come later, if we move on to IVF."

"I know that," Charley said. "I just meant…"

"I know," Savarna interjected with a grin. "It was just one of my bad puns."

In the midst of all the tests, decisions and treatments surrounding conception, Charley received a call from Dr. Liu. The sixty-year-old director of the Asian Museum had flown to India as soon as possible, but she was having a small problem.

"I'm in Thiruvananthapuram and I just left No. 10 Bingham Road. There's nobody there."

"She's probably just out on some errand. I'm sure she'll show up."

"No, there's nobody and no thing. It's vacant, totally empty. The door was open. We looked inside. Clean as a whistle."

"I don't know what to say."

"Are you sure there's no other address or news about where she could have gone?"

"None. Did you check with the neighbors?"

"Of course. I got this wonderful interpreter I found, a Mr. Sivananda. We spoke with all the neighbors. They all know Mrs. Sikand, but said she left a few weeks ago. Just took off. They have no idea why or where she was going."

"I'm so sorry."

"Yeah, me too. Are you sure Savarna hasn't gotten any other news about her grandmother's move or a new address?"

"Positive. We've been wrapped up in trying to get pregnant. If she hears anything, I'll let you know. I wish there was something I could do or some way to help."

"Yeah, well, I can't stay here forever. I'll hang out for a few more days and keep asking around. If you hear anything, please call me at this number. Oh yeah, good luck with having a baby."

Charley wrote down the number and promised two or three times that she'd call her with any news.

When Charley discussed it with Savarna that evening, Savarna said she had no idea that her grandmother had moved, but she wasn't surprised. Her parents had not given her the address when she'd visited and said her grandma didn't like people to know exactly where she was. She could always get in touch with her son and daughter-in-law and vice-a-versa, but that was by phone.

"We told Dr. Liu to not expect much," Savarna said. "It's not our fault."

"I know, but I could sure understand her excitement and disappointment. It's sort of like what we've been going through. Hope, hope, hope, then nothing."

"It's not even remotely the same. Dr. Liu knew the odds were against her."

"It seems like they're against us too."

* * * *

Pills, pills, and more pills. Savarna faithfully kept to her regimen, and Johnny was just as faithful in his donations. She had been keeping her parents in the loop and letting them know which tests and treatments she was having and what was or wasn't working. Therefore, by way of her parents and her grandmother, "all those concerned" were up to date on Savarna's exceptional and expectant attempts to conceive. Needless to say, they were broken-hearted when they realized that after a year had passed without any resulting pregnancy, that Savarna was on her last legs and was placing her final hopes on IVF. And hope was starting to lose its meaning.

She knew the process was expensive, but it really hit her how much of a financial impact it had on families when Savarna and Charley were on their fourth attempt at In Vitro Fertilization. They had agreed that this would be the last try, but not because of the money. No matter what combination of drugs they tried or how perfect the procedure had been carried out, nothing ever took. For some unexplainable reason, she could not get pregnant. Neither Dr. Mathias nor any of the other specialists and reproductive endocrinologists she consulted could explain why. They pored over all of her tests, did additional ultrasounds, including a hysterosalpingogram to re-examine the inside of her uterus and fallopian tubes and could find absolutely nothing wrong. It was frustrating and devastating. Worst of all, she didn't know how to tell her parents. If anyone could be more excited about her getting pregnant or have higher expectations than she and Charley, it was her mother and father.

* * * *

Savarna threw herself into her work and confided in Johnny, who had become extremely attached to her getting pregnant. He wouldn't admit it, but he felt a deep sense of failure and inadequacy, even though he knew, scientifically speaking, that it had nothing to do with his biology or abilities as a man.

"It's not fair," Savarna whispered one early morning, as she bent over the microscope.

"What?" Johnny said, as he continued looking over the daily checklist. "Did you say something?"

"No."

"Yes, you did. What?"

"Oh, it's stupid. I never thought I'd feel this way, but it just doesn't seem fair."

"What isn't fair?"

"Look at this," she nodded at the slide she was removing. "Mrs. McPherson. Her first IVF and bam, it takes right away! Ms. Jackson was on her second round, and we got a healthy embryo yesterday. One after another, day after day, and I'm as empty as a hollow cave. It just doesn't seem--"

"Stop right there. Don't you dare say it's not fair ever again!"

"But—"

"Come on. You know this has nothing to do with whether you're good or bad, right or wrong, or deserving or not. We've seen hundreds of people come through here. It doesn't work out for everyone, and you know it has nothing to do with whether it's fair or not. Maybe it just isn't in the cards."

"Yeah, yeah, nice speech, buddy," Savarna replied, as she got up to replace the slide and double-check the chart, "but I still 'feel' like God's checked out of the hotel or forgotten to put us on her agenda, and it doesn't seem…" Johnny cocked his head sideways and squinted disapprovingly. "Right," she concluded with a sarcastic grin.

"Feelings acknowledged and ditto. To tell you the truth, I'm glad you finally put it out there. You'd have to be a cold-hearted ass to not have it get to you. You've been working your butt off lately and living in your own world. It hasn't made the situation get any better or made you feel any different, has it?"

"Thank you, father, for I have sinned. Please accept my confession."

"Father, I wish."

They paused and silently acknowledged their situation, as the incubators hummed in the background. Johnny placed the clipboard back on the wall, hesitated, then turned just as Savarna was making her way to the phone to check in with the rest of the team.

"Hold on there, sister. What's with all this God talk? 'God checked out'? You've never believed in any of that."

Savarna hesitated and looked his way. "Did I say that?"

"You bet your Goddess you did."

"Well," she shrugged. "I have been looking a little more into this religious stuff. It's sort of hard to avoid when your partner leaves pamphlets and books out about it all over the house."

"Is she trying to convert you or something?"

"No. It's stuff my parents gave her about their teacher. She's been gobbling it up, and I've taken a peek or two. There's actually a lot of stuff he said that made sense." She turned and picked up the phone.

Johnny moved closer, so he could hear the call on the speakerphone.

"When you get enlightened or become a saint, will I notice or will you just tell me?"

"Ha ha. Very not funny."

Chapter Twenty

"So, there's an introductory session on Thursday evenings once a month and eight follow-up classes if we want to seriously consider the idea, right?" Charley double-checked with the receptionist at the county children's services office, where she had stopped on her way home from buying some new brushes and art supplies at her favorite store in Mountain View, which was just north of Sunnyvale.

"That's right," the middle-aged woman with jet-black shoulder-length hair replied. "The next orientation meeting is two weeks from yesterday, on the sixth. There's no charge and it really gives you a good, and more important, honest, overview of the process."

"Can I ask you something?"

"Absolutely. My name is May."

"OK, May. You hear all kinds of stories, right?" May nodded. "Things like 'foster kids and those up for adoption are damaged goods, they aren't really yours' and 'they don't tell you everything about them ahead of time.' How much of that is real? Are there surprises down the line? What about bonding? How much preparation and information would we have? What kind of support is there after an adoption is complete? What do we do if we don't know what to do or it's not working out?"

"Yes, yes, yes and no, yes, yes, yes, and ask for help," May responded with a chuckle and leaned forward. "Those are all excellent questions and the exact ones we answer at the orientation, to the best of our ability."

"I'm sorry," Charley said looking down at the desk, then back up at May. "It's such an overwhelming thing to think about, and I really don't know anything about it at all."

"You got that right, sister. Becoming a parent is the craziest, most overwhelming, difficult, and wonderful thing I've ever done in my life. Actually, ever do, since it never really stops."

"So, you have kids or adopted one?" Charley asked.

"Both. In fact, I think I've become a parent in most every way possible."

"How so?"

May rubbed her chin. "Let's see. First off, I became a stepmother to my husband's son, Stephen, who was four-years-old when his father and I married. Two years later we took in my brother's daughter, Melissa, who was eight when her parents went to prison for selling drugs. Then I got pregnant and had our daughter, Jillian, who just started high school this year. Last, but not least, is Jacob, who we got when he was four-years-old through the county's foster-care program and then adopted. He's a special-needs child because of his bum leg and speech difficulties. I think that's about it, for now."

"I guess it goes without saying that you know what you're talking about."

"A little. I've still got a lot to learn. It's an ongoing proposition. You keep learning stuff every day. Children are great teachers."

"Do you go to these orientation meetings?"

"Yes, as a matter of fact, I do. I always like to meet expectant parents and do what I can to make the process as clear and uncomplicated as possible. You can make a big difference in someone's life or focus on what doesn't or hasn't worked and how everything is screwed up. I like to find what works and give kids a chance to have a family like I had growing up."

"Thank you so much," Charley said. "I'll definitely try to get to one of the orientations, but I've got to figure out how to approach the whole idea with my partner first."

"You haven't spoken with him about it yet?"

"No. We're on the last IVF attempt and it doesn't seem like the right time to bring it up to her yet."

The Last Conception

"There's never a right or perfect time. It's like telling someone you want to get pregnant. Just put it out there. Tell him, sorry, I mean her, what you've been thinking about and why. You don't have to pretend to know much about it. Just say you'd like her to consider the idea. If not now, then sometime in the future."

"Thank you, May. I'll give it a shot. You've been more than helpful."

"What else is there to do? We're all here to help each other out, right? 'There but by the grace of God, go you or I.' It's not a child's fault where or to whom they are born."

"Thank you again. Hopefully I'll see you sometime soon."

* * * *

When Savarna got home that evening, she barely had time to close the door before Charley was standing in her path.

"I know this may seem brash," Charley said.

"Well, hello to you too," Savarna said, taken aback, as she made her way around Charley and sat on the couch to take off her shoes. Charley followed her step by step and sat thigh to thigh.

"You're going to say I had no right to do this," Charley continued, rubbing her hands together in her lap. "You're going to say this isn't the right time and how could I go behind your back without consulting you first. You're going to say I'm out of my mind or gone off the edge, but I did it, and I'm not sorry about it at all."

Savarna was more amused by Charley's behavior then upset, since she had no clue what had happened or what Charley was thinking in that crazy but usually insightful head of hers.

"I think we should consider adoption. I know it's too soon. We're still in the thick of IVF, and this could be the one that works, but what if it doesn't? What if this is the final straw? What if…" She stopped, when she saw Savarna's head drop and move side to side.

"I knew it." She put her arm around Savarna's shoulders. "I shouldn't have said anything. I jumped the gun. It's a crazy idea. I should drop it, forget about the whole thing."

Savarna turned her smiling face towards Charley's. "You nut. It's not too soon."

"It's not?"

Savarna put her hand on Charley's thigh. "I've been thinking about it too, but didn't want to say anything. I was afraid you would think I'd given up or was doing it to spite my parents and all their lineage mania."

"No way. That's the last thing I'd have thought. It's just that it might be the perfect alternative."

"I know. That's what I'd been thinking too. There's already a bunch of kids who need homes, and we both want a child. I know it took me awhile to come around, but I'm so into raising a child with you." They embraced. "It's never been about biology for me."

"It hasn't?" Charley leaned back, but kept hold of Savarna's hands.

"No, not in the least. It's been interesting and frustrating so far, and I'd love to experience pregnancy, but that's actually the briefest period of being a parent. When I agreed to have a baby, it was for the rest of our lives, not just to satisfy my parents and their sect."

"So, you aren't mad?"

"Do I look mad? What did I just say? I've been thinking about the same thing."

"I've actually done more than just think about it."

"What, you already found a homeless, parentless child who walked up to our door and they're in the other room waiting to call me Mommy?"

"Not quite." Charley had to laugh. "I stopped by the county children's services program today and spoke with a lady named May. There's an orientation meeting the first of each month. They answer all your questions, tell you about the process, and if you decide to go ahead they have another eight-week class you have to attend."

"Did you sign us up?"

"No, of course not. I had to talk to you first and I wasn't sure…"

"That hasn't stopped you before."

"What are you talking about?"

"Oh, just a little story I heard about someone calling the director of a museum to tell them about some items she'd been sworn to keep secret." Savarna couldn't suppress her impish grin.

"That was different. I—"

The Last Conception

"Yes, it was, and like I said before, I'm actually glad you did it, or we wouldn't know what we know now."

"It's just that… this seemed to important to wait, and I didn't know where you stood."

"I agree, and I'm relieved that it was you who said something first so I wouldn't have to." Savarna looked at Charley as if she were figuring out a puzzle. "If people only knew."

"Knew what?"

"How strong you are."

Charley held up her arm and flexed her muscles. "I am?"

"I mean your inner strength, your determination."

"Get out of here."

"No, that's why I AM here. People see us together and they think I'm the one who makes the decisions. They think I'm the one who keeps us on our feet, but it's really you. You know what you want and you go for it. You take your time to make a choice, and once you've made it, you stick with it. You know when something is right and you say so. It's like you are my subconscious or something. You *see* me and understand me better than I do myself."

Charley kissed Savarna. "If you say so."

"I know so." Savarna kissed her back.

* * * *

They had agreed to have dinner with Chitra and Mike weeks ago and almost forgot about it until Charley saw the date marked on the small floral calendar she kept in her studio by the paint-splattered easels. She called Savarna's cell and left a message to remind her that they were going to her sister's house tonight and that she'd stop and pick up a bottle of organic California red on the way.

* * * *

"Sorry I'm late," Savarna said when she knocked and let herself in Chitra and Mike's house at 7:30 that evening. "Good, you didn't wait for me."

Mike got up from the table and went toward the kitchen. "No, but I kept your food hot in the oven. Hope you like it."

"It's fabulous, Mike," Charley said loudly, so Mike could hear in the other room. "Best lasagna ever."

As Savarna threw her sweater on the back of the chair and sat down, Mike returned with a plate full of food and placed it in front of his sister-in-law.

"You outdid yourself, honey," Chitra added and gave him a kiss on the cheek.

Mike blushed.

Savarna scooped up a fork full, blew on the steaming bite a couple of times, and slowly took it in. She closed her eyes, swallowed, and smacked her lips. "Ummm. Yummy."

"When it comes to Italian, I think he's got us all beat, hands down," Charley exclaimed.

They all nodded. The women lifted their glasses of wine and Savarna toasted, "To the best cook this side of the Rockies."

"And the most handsome," Charley added.

"I'll second that." Chitra grinned and kissed Mike again.

"So, how was your day, Savarna?" Mike said quickly, to divert the attention. "Charley told us about the piece she's working on. It sounds exquisite, as usual."

"Thanks, Mike," Charley replied. "I'm not sure how it's going to turn out yet."

"Hey there, buddy," Savarna exclaimed, as she frowned at Mike. "What's with the mutual appreciation society between you and my girlfriend? If I didn't know better I'd be jealous." That got a good laugh. "Actually," Savarna continued between mouthfuls, "we had a very good day today. Long, but good."

"What was so good?" Chitra asked.

Savarna swallowed and took a sip of wine. "There's a family we've been working with for six months. They've been through the mill, if you know what I mean." She raised her eyebrows towards Charley, who nodded. "This was their third try, and they weren't sure if they could afford it again. Savarna put her hands on the table and sat up straighter. "It worked! We implanted the embryo in Mrs. Ja... excuse me, I mean, in the client, over two months ago, and she's holding her own. No sign of miscarriage or rejection in any way. Johnny and I have really been pulling for this family. They're the nicest couple you could ever meet and have wanted children so bad."

"That *is* good news," Charley agreed.

"Yes," Chitra said, with genuine feeling. "That's wonderful."

"Isn't it sort of bittersweet for you right now," Mike asked softly.

Savarna kept a smile on her face as she replied. "You could say that, but I'm trying to not think about it and keep focused on my work."

Chitra elbowed Mike in the side and gave him a look that clearly meant, "Shut up."

"You do incredible work," Chitra said quickly. "I've always been proud of you and what you do."

"Thanks, Sis." She looked at Mike. "It's OK. I don't mind you asking. In fact, there is something we wanted to talk with you about."

"Yeah," Charley said. "I wanted to wait until Savarna got here before bringing it up."

"Really," Chitra said. She and Mike glanced at each other. "We wanted to ask you about something too."

"What was that?" Savarna asked.

"Go ahead," Mike said. "What's so big you had to wait for Savarna?"

"Well, two things really."

"And they are…?" Chitra asked.

"It's hasn't worked," Savarna said quickly. "Nothing has worked."

"You don't know that yet," Charley exclaimed.

"OK, you're right. So far, nothing has worked," Savarna said.

"You mean…" Chitra said.

"Yes, IVF," Savarna finished her sentence.

"So, there's still a chance, right?" Mike chimed.

"There's always a chance," Savarna replied, "but this is our sixth try and something is not right. Nothing is taking hold."

"Nobody knows why," Charley interjected. "She's had every test up the wazoo."

"And she literally means up the wazoo," Savarna said, grinning.

"OK, OK," Mike chuckled. "I get the picture."

"I hope not," Savarna said, as everyone laughed.

"So," Chitra said softly, "if this doesn't work, and I understand that there's still a chance, but if it doesn't, what are you going to do?"

"That's what we wanted to ask you," Savarna replied. "It's not as much what do we do, as how do I tell Mom and Dad? You know what this means to them and all the others. I don't want to let them down, but obviously, we may not have any choice in the matter."

"Well… that's a difficult question," Chitra said and looked to Mike for support.

"If you don't mind me asking," Savarna said, "how did you tell them after you found out you couldn't have children?"

"That was tough," Mike said, as he lowered his head. "That was real tough, but not as hard as hearing it ourselves."

Chitra hugged Mike around the shoulders and said, "They did better than I thought they would, really. I've got to give them credit. It was a big blow for them as well as us." She turned to Savarna and Charley, while keeping her arm around Mike. "Mom was very understanding. I could tell she was just as sad for me as she was for herself and Dad… he just hugged me and cried."

A brief silence transpired, then Savarna spoke delicately. "This is a little different. I don't mean to minimize it in the slightest or how painful it was and still must be, but I've got Mom and Dad, their religious beliefs, and a long line of zealots who are expecting me to produce the goods, so… there's a little bit of pressure."

Chitra sat up straight. "Just tell them. They can handle it."

"Damn the torpedoes, all ahead," Mike added.

"We've had a lot of torpedoes, Mike, and none of them seem to have worked," Charley said, trying to lighten things up a little.

"Torpedoes?" Savarna looked puzzled. "I've never heard them called…"

"Anyway," Chitra said, "we can come with you, if that will help."

"Safety in numbers," Mike exclaimed.

"OK, enough with the clichés," Chitra chided her husband. "He's right though. It will be more difficult for them to say anything with me there."

"Would you really?" Savarna said.

"Absolutely," Chitra said

"That would be fabulous, Sis," said Savarna. "Are you sure?"

"Yes," Chitra replied, reaching her hand across the table and grabbing Savarna's. "Without a doubt."

"This is still all hypothetical, right?" Charley interjected. "This last embryo might be the one, for all we know."

"Of course," Mike said.

"Of course," Savarna added, without much conviction. "There's still a chance."

"Yes," Chitra said. "There is still a chance, and we pray that it works, but if for any reason it doesn't happen and you want us to support you in telling Mom and Dad, I just thought of the perfect time."

"When would that—" Savarna cut herself short. "Oh my God. You are so right. I know exactly what you're thinking."

"Can you two fill us in?" Mike asked.

The sisters looked at one another and then Savarna explained. "At the end of next month is a special festival."

"More like a small group party," Chitra corrected.

"Yeah," Savarna continued, "more like a party for a small gathering of followers."

"They have this once a year, and it's primarily used as a means to remember the core principles of love, being of service, and forgiving yourself and others," Chitra explained.

"What better time to spill the beans?" Savarna concluded. "Right after the ceremony, when they'll be in a good mood."

"Who's got the brains now, Big Sis?" Chitra smiled.

"The one and only amazing Little Sis, that's who." Savarna smiled back.

"Well," Mike said, getting up to clear the dishes. "Can you hand me your—"

"You sit back down," Charley said firmly. "Whoever cooks is not allowed to do the dishes, period."

"Yes, ma'm," Mike grinned, as Chitra grabbed his sleeve and pulled him back into his chair. "Now that that's settled, what else was it you wanted to ask?"

Savarna and Charley looked confused.

"You said there were two things you wanted to ask us."

"Oh, yes," Charley said, "that."

"Yes," Savarna nodded. "That. Well, we've been thinking about... actually, it was Charley who got the ball rolling, but we've been looking into the idea... if I can't get pregnant... of maybe, perhaps..."

"Adopting," Charley finished.

Chitra and Mike didn't say a word but sat silently and looked at one another. Charley and Savarna couldn't tell what they were thinking or how they were taking this.

"We were wondering what you thought about the idea," Savarna said, waiting anxiously for some response.

Mike and Chitra stared across the table at their guests.

"Oh my God!" exclaimed Chitra, as Mike shook his head side to side. "You've got to be kidding."

Savarna and Charley exchanged a look of concern.

"What?" Charley said. "Did we say something wrong?"

Chitra and Mike couldn't keep a straight face any longer, and both broke out in grins that could have been used for Happy Face posters. "That's what we were going to talk with you about!" Chitra almost shouted. "We've been thinking about the same thing."

"Actually," Mike said, "we've been doing more than just thinking about it. We've already put in our application and have had four interviews with Homes Beyond Borders."

This time it was Savarna and Charley who remained silent, both of them wide-eyed with jaws dropped.

"Oh, my, Goddess!" Charley finally said. "That's fantastic."

Savarna closed, then opened her mouth. "When... how... why?"

"Details...details," Charley demanded with glee.

"It's something we talked about when we first got together. We've been thinking about it for years," Mike explained. "Even before Chitra's cancer and everything, we had agreed to adopt a child. We'd just planned on having one the old-fashioned way first. So, when that didn't work out, we decided to go ahead," Mike explained.

"Not right away," Chitra added.

"Well, no," Mike said. "It took you...us...a while to recover from that punch in the gut."

"Of course," Charley understood. "How many more interviews or classes or whatever before it's a go?"

"Next up is a home assessment and visit and then one more final interview with the entire staff," Mike said.

"They've been fantastic," Chitra said, "every step of the way. Not a sour note in the whole process."

"It's not cheap," Mike followed up.

"Tell us about it," Savarna said. "It's probably similar to IVF."

"We might have to wait a while," Chitra said. "We asked for a baby from India, and they said that takes longer. There's more red tape there than some countries."

"Why India?" Savarna asked.

"Why not?" Mike replied.

"It just felt right to us, our heritage and all and Mom and Dad, you know?" Chitra said.

"Yeah, I get that," Savarna said, nodding.

"Well," Charley raised her glass. "A toast to the soon-to-be new parents. Congratulations and good luck."

Their glasses all rang as they touched.

"Oh yeah, speaking of Mom and Dad," Savarna said, after taking a small sip, "when are you going to tell them about all this?"

Chitra fidgeted in her chair and quickly glanced at Mike, who answered for her. "We already did."

"You did?" Savarna exclaimed. "When?!"

"About three weeks ago," Mike replied. "Once we were pretty sure everything was going to go through."

"They made us promise not to say anything," Chitra quickly added as she leaned toward Savarna. "They didn't want to 'upset' you or 'get you off track,' they said."

"How would that have made any difference?" Savarna asked.

"I know, it doesn't make sense," Chitra said, "but they were almost beside themselves convincing us to keep it quiet. We promised not to say anything until after you were pregnant. I think Mom thought it would somehow jinx the whole thing if we said something to you."

"That's just stupid," Savarna exclaimed. "She still believes I'm going to have a baby, regardless of reality or the present odds. It doesn't make sense."

"Yes, it does," Charley said quietly. "Your parents' entire lives are wrapped up in this lineage mentality. If they allow the slightest crack in their armor it could jeopardize their entire belief system and threaten the very fabric of what they and generations before them have strived to maintain and follow."

"But the essence of what he taught had nothing to do with heredity or bloodlines."

"You know that and I know that," Charley said, "and I think they know that in some part of their consciousness as well, but it's not something that will change like the weather or that they'll let go of easily."

"She's right," Chitra said.

"Probably," Savarna replied. "But you still should have told us."

"Now you're right," Chitra smiled. "We should have, but we didn't, and now we have."

Charley got up, picked up her plate, and stacked the others on top. Savarna helped her with the glasses.

"What about you," Chitra asked. "Are you planning on adopting a baby, if it comes down to that?"

"No, we're thinking probably a three to five-year-old through the county adoption program," Savarna said, as she walked toward the kitchen."

"That's where we're going for the classes," Charley added, as she followed Savarna into the kitchen.

Mike and Chitra collected the rest of the dinner utensils and put them in the sink, where Charley had already started to rinse and hand them to Savarna to place in the dishwasher.

"Boy or girl," Chitra asked.

"Either one," Charley said.

"We don't have any preference," Savarna said. "What about you?"

"Girls have it rough in India, so we told them we'd prefer a girl," Chitra said.

The Last Conception

Savarna closed the dishwasher, turned around, and leaned against the countertop. Charley dried her hands, stood next to Savarna, and put her arm around her shoulder. Chitra approached them and encircled them both in a hug.

"Get over here," Charley insisted, waving for Mike to join them.

Chitra said, "We are so blessed to have you in our lives."

"And you," Savarna said.

"This is family," Charley added. "And I am so grateful that we have a choice."

Chapter Twenty-One

Savarna received the results from the last round of IVF at the doctor's office on her way home from work four weeks later. She had told Doctor Mathias that she didn't want to talk about it but just wanted to pick up the report. She almost opened the sealed manila envelope in the car but slapped her own hand. This was something she and Charley had to see together.

When she got home she placed the envelope on the dining room table, fixed herself a cup of coffee, and waited until Charley got back from her studio, where she'd had to finish a picture that had been commissioned and she'd promised would be done by the next day. Savarna had one cup after another until she was pacing like a cougar in heat.

"Damn!" She spilled some of her drink on her slacks. She was in the kitchen with a cold wet towel trying to wash off the stain and save her pants, when Charley barged through the door and threw a large picture frame on the couch.

"Did you get it?"

Savarna nodded toward the table and hung up the dishtowel. "Well, what do you think?"

Charley sat down and took the envelope in her hands. "Any gut feeling or premonition?"

"Nothing, one way or the other," Savarna replied, as she came up behind Charley and rested her hands on her shoulders. "Just open it. I've been going nuts waiting for you to get here."

"Sorry," Charley apologized. "The last color combination in the

The Last Conception

corner wasn't quite right, and it kept bleeding into—"

"Open it, for God's sake!"

Charley slid her finger into the upper edge of the envelope and loosened the flap. She felt Savarna's fingers tighten when she pulled out the form. She held it up and started reading to herself, as Savarna looked over her shoulder. Before Charley could finish the summary, Savarna left and went to their bedroom. Charley read to the end and let the paper drop from her hands, tears dropping down her cheeks. She went to be with Savarna, who was lying on their bed with tears dripping down her face onto the pillow. Charley lay down behind Savarna and spooned her in an embrace.

"I guess I wanted this baby more than I ever realized." Savarna sniffled.

"I'm so sorry. I wish I could fix it."

"It's beyond repair. We're finished."

Chapter Twenty-Two

"We are so glad you came this year," their mother said, from the front seat of their parents' car. "It was a wonderful service and always good to remember our roots."

Savarna and Chitra sat next to each other in the back seat and shared a sheepish grin.

"Yes," their father added. "Since you've both grown up, you've never shown much interest, but it was good to have us all together again and for the others to see you there." He looked in the rearview mirror at Savarna.

"I've gotten more interested since we've been trying to get pregnant," Savarna answered. "I've been reading some of the books you gave Charley and wanted to get a better feel for the whole thing. See what it's all about."

"And," Mr. Sikand said, "what do you think?"

"When it comes down to it, wasn't he saying be kind to others, pay attention, and become the peace and love you seek?"

"Exactly," her father grinned proudly. "He said we're all one and the same. There is only a sense of separation, but not really."

"Yes," Chitra said. "I get that too, but what really got me today was the whole focus on forgiveness and compassion, the part about not always getting what we want. Isn't that what Mrs. Banarjee was saying?"

"Ah, you listened well," her mother replied. "You are both such smart girls."

"Everyone knows we get it from our parents," Chitra said.

Their father laughed and said, "I'm sure all your smart genes came from your mother. She's the brains of the family."

Mrs. Sikand playfully slapped her husband on the shoulder. "I think it actually skipped a generation and came from your mother. She never went to college, but there's a way about her that you know she knows what she knows. If you know what I mean?"

"That's a lot of knowing going on," Savarna said and laughed along with everyone else. "Speaking of knowing." She glanced at her sister, who nodded the go-ahead. "There's something I need you both to know."

"We already know about you and Charley," her father said, smiling, "so it can't be that earth shaking. What is it?"

"Well, I don't know where it falls on the earth shaking scale, but it's a huge turning point in our lives."

Their mother and father stopped grinning. Davidia looked in the rearview mirror, and Mira turned around in her seat. Savarna looked to Chitra once again for reassurance, which she got, and proceeded with caution.

"You know we've been trying to get pregnant for almost a year now." Neither parent said a word. "We've tried everything, including six rounds of IVF. I've had every test known to womankind, and nobody can figure out why I can't get pregnant, but I can't. Our last round was the final attempt. We're going to have to let it go."

"What?" Mira exclaimed. She grabbed her husband's shoulder. "Pull over!"

"Mom," Chitra said, "calm down."

"I said pull over, and don't you tell me to calm down." Mr. Sikand did as he was instructed, as soon as there was a safe place to park. "What do you mean you have to 'let it go?' You can't."

"It's not a matter of whether we can or can't," Savarna replied, trying to keep her cool. "It is simply the reality of our situation. Believe me, I've wanted this as much as you."

"No, you haven't!" her mother exploded. "You have no idea how many people are depending on you. It's not about you. It's about the next generation."

"I'm sorry I'm such a disappointment, but I can't help it!"

"You can keep trying," Mrs. Sikand insisted. "You can keep at it until it's successful."

"I'm not a machine, Mom! Just because you believe it will happen doesn't always make it so."

"Remember what they said today," Chittra said protectively, "about letting go and forgiving?"

"Yes, I do," Mr. Sikand said, as Mrs. Sikand crossed her arms and seethed. "But she was talking about life in general, not this specific situation."

"That's baloney, Dad," Savarna replied. "She said if it can't be applied in everyday life with everyday problems, then it probably wasn't the truth and not worth practicing."

"Yes, that's all very well and good," Mrs. Sikand stated, "but the very essence of the lineage, which Mrs. Banarjee follows, depends on the bloodline of our teacher being continued, and you are—"

"No, it's not!" Savarna interrupted. "I don't remember reading anything anywhere or being told in any meeting or gathering that that was a requirement or tenet of his teachings."

"Of course not," her father said. "It's an unwritten, but well understood spiritual law that has been passed from one generation to another. Nobody says it out loud or talks about it and you know why."

"It's secret," Chitra answered, as her father nodded.

"Isn't that convenient," Savarna added.

"Savarna," Mrs. Sikand said, uncrossing her arms and laying her hand on Savarna's knee. "I'm sorry I overreacted, but please, please keep trying."

"I can't and I won't," Savarna replied. "It's over. Let it go."

Her mother turned around, as tears washed over her and her husband's faces.

"There's something else," Savarna whispered, not sure if they were listening any longer. "We're looking into adoption."

"It's not the same," her mother answered. "And you know it."

"What about us?" Chitra exclaimed. "You and Dad both gave Mike and me your blessing and said you were thrilled that we were going to adopt."

"Chitra!" her father said quickly. "You were not supposed to—"

"We already know, Dad," Savarna said.

The Last Conception

"You know?" Mr. Sikand asked. Savarna nodded.

"That's different," Mrs. Sikand finally said. "A totally different situation."

"Mom," Savarna said as calmly as she could, "we're not any different than Chitra and Mike. We both want the same thing."

"She's right, Mom," Chitra added.

"Stop making me into something I'm not," Savarna said.

Silence reigned for the rest of the ride, as the Sikands dropped each of their daughters off at their respective homes. Savarna and Chitra had never seen their parents act like this. They prayed they'd understand, but didn't know if they ever would or could.

Chapter Twenty-Three

Two weeks went by without a word. Savarna checked in with her sister. She said she'd not had a single call from their parents and she'd left a number of messages. Savarna said she'd done the same. They knew they couldn't avoid them much longer, since the party they'd planned for their parent's fortieth wedding anniversary was the upcoming Friday night and had been arranged well in advance. They had rented a social hall at the Hindu temple in Palo Alto and invited over twenty guests and their families. The temple had fond memories for their parents, as it was the first place they met new friends upon their arrival in the States. The congregation welcomed people of all faiths and had been helpful with community connections and support, even though the Sikands were not Hindu. The social hall was the perfect size and wasn't as overwhelming as the primary room of worship.

Before they knew it, the anniversary day was upon them.

"You look beautiful," Savarna reassured Charley, as she and Chitra admired her in her light blue-and-gold-trimmed sari.

"Like an Indian princess," Chittra added.

"I wouldn't go that far," Savarna laughed. "Unless we get a wig, it will be a little difficult to transform her short blond hair into a long black braid."

Charley blushed, then looked at her arms. "I really like these bangles and earrings," she said as she felt the long dangling silver connected to her ears. "Thank you for letting me wear all this."

"We're lucky that it all fit," Chitra said. "I thought we were close to the same size, and it looks like it's going to work."

The Last Conception

"Thank God," Savarna added. "We only have three or four of these things between us." Chitra was wearing an orange-and-yellow-patterned wrap, which resembled Savarna's in cut and length, but was not the same purple tone with small stitched lotus flowers on the hem.

"Are you sure this is OK?" Charley asked for the umpteenth time.

"Even if it wasn't," Savarna replied, "and it is, I'd still bring you anyway."

"Absolutely," Chitra said. "You are part of this family and always will be."

"Besides," Savarna said, "I'm the one they're mad at, not you."

"They aren't mad," Chitra corrected. "They're hurt and disappointed."

"It's not about you," Charley consoled. "It's the religious belief they've lived for so long."

"Yeah," Savarna said with a frown, "and it just so happens that my ability to procreate is the blood and guts of the whole charade."

"Come on," Chitra said, pulling Savarna and Charley by their sleeves toward the bedroom door. "Let's show Mike."

Mike had been patiently waiting for the ladies to appear so they could get to the anniversary party on time. He had hired the caterers and was in charge of the schedule.

He had seen Savarna and Chitra all dolled up in their traditional dress before, but it still got to him every time. He actually wished they would wear them more often, but Chitra said they were such a hassle and didn't really work for a lot of day-to-day activities.

"Wow!" he exclaimed, when they came into the living room. "You all look incredibly gorgeous."

"Thank you," Chitra replied. "You don't look bad yourself."

Mike was dressed in a white blue-embroidered cotton Nehru jacket and matching slacks.

"Better watch out," Savarna chided. "Someone might mistake you for Shahrukh Khan."

The sisters laughed.

"Who's Shahrukh Khan?" Charley asked.

"He's one of the most famous actors in India," Mike explained. "And there's no comparison. I'm much better looking."

Chitra went up to Mike and gave him a kiss. "I think so."

"Ladies," Mike said, bowing slightly, "after you."

As they got ready to leave, Charley exclaimed, "Wait. I've got to get the card I made for them." She ran to the room and came back with a large envelope. "OK, let's celebrate."

"Let's see if they've disowned me or not," Savarna said. The door closed behind them.

* * * *

They arrived in plenty of time. Mike checked to make sure everything was in place. Beautiful white and purple tablecloths draped the tables. There were plenty of chairs, plates, napkins, and silverware, and the caterers were bringing out the covered food and placing the variety of aromatic dishes on the serving table. Chitra took out the large framed photograph she'd brought of her parents on their wedding day and placed it on the stand that Charley had provided. As the first guests arrived, the dancers and accompanying musicians went into the back room to change and prepare for their performance. Mike had gauged accurately that the hall was small enough to not require a microphone.

Savarna, Chitra, Mike, and Charley greeted everyone at the door and invited them to place their gifts on the small altar table next to the photo and help themselves to the hot food. Music quietly played in the background on a portable CD player Chitra had rented.

"It's almost seven and they still aren't here," Savarna whispered to Chitra, after introducing her mother's friend Satya, of Satya's Tea Room, and her husband, to Charlemagne, the name Charley asked Savarna to use in this situation. Mrs. Muktananda from their father's store and her husband and grown son were the next to arrive and make their way to dinner.

"They'll be here," Chitra said, trying to reassure herself as much as her sister.

"Come on," Mike interjected. "There's no way they'd miss… look." He nodded toward the doorway, which Mr. and Mrs. Sikand had just entered wearing modest but refined Indian dress, including a head wrap for their father. As soon as the guests turned and saw that the celebrated couple had arrived, they all clapped. The Sikands placed their palms together in front of their hearts and bowed to one and all. They hugged Savarna and Chitra and shook hands with Charley but didn't look any of them in the eye.

"Mr. and Mrs. Sikand," Mike said, as he put out his arm for Mrs. Sikand. "Let me lead you to your place of honor."

"So, it's going to be like this," Savarna said to Chitra and Charley. "I thought they would have cooled down by now."

The widowed spiritual teacher, Mrs. Banarjee, came in by herself right after the girls went to get food for their parents and mingle at the tables. She helped herself to a small plate of rice and sat down quietly in an end-table chair. Other guests at her table nodded and smiled to acknowledge her presence.

After bellies were filled with food and ears with laughter and conversation, Mike introduced the dancers.

"And now, in honor of Mr. and Mrs. Sikand's fortieth wedding anniversary, we bring you the Karang Dancers."

Several tablas beat a rhythm as the entertainers made their way to the center of the hall and the musicians sat on the provided carpet. One beautiful dancer after another moved first alone and then in unison in front of the guests, as Mr. and Mrs. Sikand clapped their hands in delight.

"What kind of dance is that?" Charley asked, after they had gotten their food and joined their parents at the head table.

"It's called Kathakali," Mike answered.

"It's a traditional kind of dance from southern India," Savarna added. "That's where Mom and Dad grew up, even though their families are not from that region."

"Each dance tells a story," Mike explained.

A male and female dancer began a series of movements close together. They alternated between stepping away and towards one another.

"I don't have to tell you what this one's about," Mike chuckled.

Savarna kept looking at her parents for some clue, but they were smiling and watching the dancers, without any acknowledgment or glance in her direction. Charley noticed her partner's apprehension and sadness. "Hey," she said, "have a little faith."

"Faith," Savarna replied, "that's what got us into this mess in the first place."

"No," Charley replied. "It wasn't faith, it was hope. Blind hope."

"Are you defending them?"

"No, just trying to understand."

* * * *

The dancing lasted for about an hour. The entertainers received a standing ovation. Then the speeches began. Everyone praised the Sikands for their commitment, generosity, and family values. Just as Mike was about to ask Mira and Davidia to speak, Mrs. Banarjee arose.

"Mike," Chitra said and nodded at Mrs. Banarjee. He turned and saw her standing and immediately sat down.

"You know I don't usually attend public gatherings like this, let alone have something to say," Mrs. Banarjee began. "This, however, is a special occasion and it's not solely a result of Mr. and Mrs. Sikand's union forty years ago to this day. Everyone here knows the kindness and devotion that this couple have lived throughout their lives together, and most of you know their daughters, Chitra and Savarna." The guests followed Mrs. Banarjee's gaze and smiled at the two sisters. "It is through the lives of their girls and the women they have become that Mira and Davidia are truly honored. They have been such a blessing, not only to them, but to us all."

"That's for sure," Mike whispered to Chitra.

"We often live out our dreams through our children," Mrs. Banarjee continued. "And these girls are truly a dream come true." Chitra blushed and hid her face, but Savarna kept listening with every fiber of her being. "We are not all so lucky or as blessed to have such offspring or have them live such long, fulfilling lives." Mira and Davidia were both holding back their tears. "Even so, the most wonderful children in the world cannot fulfill every dream or hope we have guarded in our hearts. There are events over which they have no control. There are choices made for them that were not theirs.

"Davidia and Mira Sikand. Today is not only a day to honor and pay our respects to you, but also express our love and gratitude to the children you have before you. The ones that are in your life now. The

The Last Conception

daughters who are expressions of everything our Teacher has ever taught."

Mrs. Banarjee sat down. Everyone clapped for both generations of Sikands, while the Sikands themselves were all unabashedly awash in tears, along with Charley and Mike.

When the clapping stopped, Mr. Sikand slowly rose, wiped his eyes with his napkin, and said, "Thank you all for helping us celebrate our fortieth wedding anniversary and being such supportive family and friends. It doesn't really mean anything unless you have people like you to share it with." He turned toward his daughters. "And you... what can I add to what Mrs. Banarjee has said? You are everything to us... everything. There is nobody in this world that makes us more proud and grateful to be alive."

Mrs. Sikand, who had been staring blankly ahead ever since Mrs. Banarjee had spoken, suddenly pulled her husband by his sleeve and nodded for him to sit down, which he did, though taken aback and confused.

Mira stood and stared straight at her daughters. "I want to apologize to both of you. I love you more than the air I breathe and have never wanted to hurt you in any way." She took a sip of water then continued as the rest of the guests remained silent, trying to hear what was being said, though not understanding what it was all about. "Savarna, I've been so wrapped up in the past and future, that I forgot to see what was right in front of my eyes. Please forgive me."

As soon as the shock wore off, which was but a second, Savarna and Chitra jumped out of their seats and quickly went to embrace their parents. Not knowing exactly what to do, the rest of those attending clapped once again. Mike stood and made a toast and everyone joined him.

"To the Sikands, the best and only in-laws I've ever known. All I can say is thank God you two got together and a thousand blessings for your marriage today and another forty years."

The musicians, who had taken a break to eat, regrouped and started to play a fast raga, as everyone else approached the couple to offer their congratulations. By the time all the Sikands went to thank Mrs. Banarjee for her words, they discovered she had already left.

A short time later, as Chitra and the rest of the revelers were teaching Mike and Charley how to dance a popular Bollywood number being played by the quartet, Mrs. Sikand pulled Savarna to the side of the crowd.

"I'm sorry."

"That's OK, Mom."

"I guess your father and I shouldn't have talked to Mrs. Banarjee about our situation. Well, actually, I'm glad we did. She was right. It's what's here and now that's the most important and how we treat one another."

"Mom. I can only do what I can do. I know you're disappointed, but…"

"Listen, will you do just one little thing?"

Savarna nodded, as her mother took her hands in hers.

"If we pay for it, will you try that IVF thing a couple more times, just in case?"

"Mom!" Savarna said with a scowl and paused to consider her request. "I'll think about it, OK? That's all I can promise."

Mrs. Sikand put her arm around Savarna's waist. "That's all I'm asking. Now, tell me more about this whole adoption thing."

Chapter Twenty-Four

Savarna took the paddle out of the slot in the front of the car and put it back in the charger on the wall, while Charley opened the garage door.

"I'm so excited, I can hardly stand it," Charley said with delight, as they accelerated onto the freeway.

"Luckily, you're sitting it," Savarna said, as Charley rolled her eyes. "You know the only person that could be more thrilled is me and maybe my parents."

"Don't drive too fast. It would really mess things up if you got a ticket or we were in an accident."

"Oh, really. I didn't know that."

"You are driving a little fast."

"Yes, Mother, I'll slow down."

"Ha ha."

"Actually, will you give my mom a call and let her know we're on our way and should be there in about fifteen minutes? The traffic's not too bad."

Savarna handed Charley her cell phone. "Dial number two."

"Who's number one?"

"As if you didn't know."

Charley pressed the speed dial. Mrs. Sikand answered after just one ring.

"Savarna, we've been here for an hour already."

"Hi, Mrs. Sikand. This is Charley. Savarna's driving and can't use the phone."

"Oh, hi Charley. Where are you?"

"The traffic's not bad. We should be there in fifteen minutes, she said."

"Well, it's about time. Tell my daughter that we've already been waiting an hour."

Charley had the phone on speaker, so Savarna heard every word.

"Tell her their flight doesn't arrive until 2:30, that's another half hour."

"Savarna says there's still plenty of time until they arrive. We'll see you soon."

"OK, thanks for calling."

"Bye."

Charley hung up the phone.

"Guess who's the most excited now?" Savarna said. "I can't believe they've already been there waiting for over an hour. Did they think that would make the plane land any sooner?"

"I hope they don't mind me coming."

"I can't believe you said that."

"Well, it is a family thing, and I'm not always sure where I stand."

"You ARE part of the family, and don't ever doubt it."

"OK. My lips are sealed."

"Remember that card you made for their anniversary party eight months ago?"

"Yeah."

"They had it framed and it's hanging on the wall in their hallway."

"Really?"

"Last time I was over Dad made a point of showing me how nicely the frame matched your beautiful watercolor of the couple floating together above the lily pond you painted on the front cover."

"They framed it and hung it?"

"Yes indeed, and you know what else?"

"More?"

"He also showed me the picture of you and me together, you know, the one taken at their anniversary by Mike?"

"A picture of us, together?"

"Yep, right next to your painting."

"That's so sweet. I had no idea."

The Last Conception

* * * *

Savarna and Charley pulled into the short-term parking at San Jose Airport twenty minutes later and made their way to the Virgin Airlines waiting area for arriving flights, where they found Mr. and Mrs. Sikand anxiously watching every passenger who disembarked from the previous flight.

"Mom. Dad. Sit down," Savarna said. "That flight is from Boston. Theirs isn't for another twenty or thirty minutes."

The Sikand's sat briefly but were on their feet two minutes later. Savarna wasn't able to sit much longer either.

Fifty minutes later there was still no sign of them. The Sikands went up to the woman at the airline desk and asked what on earth was taking so long.

"They ran into some head winds that caused a slight delay. They should be arriving any moment now."

"Well, I certainly hope so," Mr. Sikand said. "It would have been nice…"

"Savarna!" Charley yelled, as she grabbed her shoulder. "Savarna! They're here!"

Savarna and her parents turned around, as a throng of passengers disembarked through the gate.

"Chitra!" Mrs. Sikand exclaimed. They all saw Mike and Chitra making their way toward them, carrying a number of bags and a bundle in Chitra's arms.

Hugs and kisses were given and received.

"Here she is," Chitra cooed blissfully, unwrapping the blanket that surrounded the two-month-old infant. "Your granddaughter, Satya Sikand Nolan."

"She's beautiful!" Savarna exclaimed.

"Gorgeous," Charley joyfully chimed in.

"A princess," Mrs. Sikand added, as she kissed the sleeping baby's forehead, and the baby raised an eyebrow and smiled in her sleep.

Mr. Sikand was so moved he just stood staring and had nothing to say. The tears streaming down his face said it all.

"Look at all that black hair," Savarna said. "There's enough there for a wig."

"She looks just like you, Mike," Charley said. They all turned toward Charley with looks of dismay. "I was just… I'm sorry." Then Mike and the rest of the family burst out laughing.

"Yes, exactly," Mike replied. "I think it's her nose."

"You must be exhausted," Savarna said and led them to a waiting area, where they all sat down.

"Mom, do you want to hold her?" Chitra asked, as she handed Satya to her grandmother.

Their mother gently cradled the precious little girl.

* * * *

Mike and Chitra had been in Mumbai for the last three weeks, going through the final process with the international agency and Indian government to adopt Satya. They'd been informed that there was a baby available, but they would have to travel to India immediately. They were informed of this on a Wednesday and had only two days to prepare. They'd been told they might have to travel at the drop of a hat by their social worker, but hadn't realized the hat was already falling at the time they were told.

Once they'd arrived they had been taken directly to the orphanage and introduced to the baby girl who had been left at the center's doorstep the week before. Then came the long hurry up and wait. They stayed with the baby in a hotel close by and accompanied one official after another to government offices in every part of the city. Eventually they had to fly to Delhi and back for the final papers.

* * * *

"Mom," Savarna said, "can I?" She motioned toward Satya.

Her mother slowly handed the baby to her daughter. Charley moved in tight next to Savarna, so they were practically holding Satya together.

"Mom," Savarna said, smiling, "we're going to have to work out a schedule. If you're lucky we'll let you and Dad have her occasionally, but she's going to be at her Aunt Savarna's house all the time."

"No way," her father replied. "We have priority. We are her grandparents." Mr. Sikand put out his arms, wanting to hold Satya. "It's my turn."

"I can see we're going to have to fight you about this," Savarna grinned, as she handed her father his granddaughter.

"No need to fight about it," Mike said with a smile. "We can use the help. We're exhausted."

"Of course you are," Charley said. "Anybody would be, even without a baby. The time difference alone is enough to wipe me out."

"Let's go home," Mike whispered to Chitra.

"Here," Mr. Sikand said, handing Satya to Chitra. "I think we should let her go home with her parents tonight, don't you?"

Chapter Twenty-Five

"What a lovely show," Charley's mother exclaimed, as she came up behind her daughter at her exhibit in Rhiannon's gallery.

"Thank you, Mom." Charley turned and swung her arms around her mother's shoulders. "I'm so glad you could make it. There are drinks and sweets around the corner. She started to lead her mother there.

"I don't need any sweets, thank you. I came to see your work and to talk with you about something."

Charley nodded at the painting in front of them and several others around the room. "You've seen most of these already, but there might be a couple new ones."

"What's this?" her mother said, frowning slightly, nodding at a painting a few feet away to her right. "That doesn't look familiar."

"Oh that. That's a piece I did last month."

They moved over a few feet, as her mother leaned closer and admired the painting.

"This is beautiful."

"Thanks, Mom. Glad you like it."

"Like it. I love this."

"You've said that about everything I've ever done since kindergarten, Mom, and I never get tired of hearing it."

Her mother laughed. "Maybe, but this is especially good. Is that two women floating above the landscape or a shadow of one?"

"It's two women."

"And is that faint blue-green image coming through the trees a child?"

The Last Conception

"Could be." Charley grinned.

"I wonder what inspired this?" she asked.

"I wonder," Charley replied.

Ms. Burnell moved closer to her daughter and whispered, "That's actually what I wanted to talk with you about."

"Hey, I thought you came to admire my masterpieces!" Charley said.

"I did indeed and—"

"Well, unless you have to rush off to some big court case or something, why don't you look around first and see if there's anything else you haven't seen?"

"No big court cases, dear. Very few things ever get to that stage. We usually work things out well in advance."

"Here," Charley said, taking her mother's hand. "This will send further shock waves up your spine." She led her to the back of the foyer, where her painting of a sensually revealing orchid was mounted.

"Well, this is something. What gorgeous colors and detail. It must have taken you a while to create this."

"Much longer than I thought," Charley confirmed.

"I guess some things take longer than we expect, don't they? Especially when it comes to creation."

"Yes, Mom. They do. You definitely don't beat around the bush, do you? It seems that I'm not the only one whose mind is on children and creation."

"You got me there. That's what I wanted to speak with you about. Is there somewhere we can go?"

"I thought so," Charley said. "Follow me."

Charley and her mother went out onto the small patio behind the gallery and sat on two folding chairs in the middle of some potter's wheels, workbenches, and empty picture stands.

"How's the adoption process going?"

"Funny you should ask just now. Well, I guess it's not that funny, but we're almost done with our last class and we've already had our home study approved. There's a little boy they've suggested we might get to meet in a few weeks."

Ms. Burnell hugged her daughter. "That's wonderful, absolutely wonderful! What's the boy's name?"

"They said his name is Sid and he's five-and-a-half-years old."

"Do you know anything else about him?"

"No," Charley said, "absolutely nothing. Social services haven't been as easy or forthcoming as they said they would be in the beginning. They change dates all the time, ask us to repeat stuff we've already done, change workers or cancel meetings. Sometimes it doesn't seem like anybody there knows what anybody else is doing and we're usually the last to be informed, if we are at all. Instead of supporting us in the process it seems like they're fighting against us." Charley dropped her chin for a moment and looked at her feet, then jerked her head up and smiled. "It will all work out. I know it will. Whatever is supposed to be will be."

Ms. Burnell put her hand on Charley's knee. "Absolutely. I'm sure it will. I can't wait to meet Sid, if that happens."

"So, what is it?" Charley asked, cocking her head sideways. "What did you want to see me about, besides all my wonderful paintings, of course?"

"They are wonderful."

"Mom?"

Pausing and gazing up at the ivy-covered brick wall behind her, Ms. Burnell took a deep breath and looked back at her daughter.

"Now, don't think this is crazy and I hope you won't think I'm meddling or anything. This is just an idea."

"Mom?"

"I know how much you and Savarna want to have a biological child and, believe me, I know what that desire is like," she said, squeezing Charley's hands. "And I know how much it means to Savarna and her parents for her to bear and birth a child."

"You don't know the half of it, Mom."

"Well, I was thinking… actually I was sleeping and woke up with the idea. It was almost like a dream, but it wasn't. Do you know what I mean?"

"Yes, some of my paintings come to me like that." Charley waited expectantly.

"Why don't you take one of Savarna's eggs and some sperm from…

who's your friend... John?"

"Johnny?"

"Yeah, Johnny. Take Savarna's egg and his sperm, get them together in the lab, then implant the fertilized egg inside you and have you carry the child to term."

Charley's eyes widened.

"Me... have me carry our child?"

"That's possible, isn't it? They could do that, couldn't they?"

"Well, theoretically yes, but... me?"

"Why not? You've wanted this as long as I can remember and if it's not working with Savarna..."

"It's always been her. We decided right from the beginning that it would be her and the lineage and all that." Charley looked at her knees. "I don't know."

"The lineage? What lineage? What's that got to do with anything?"

Charley quickly looked up. "Nothing. Well, actually it is something, in fact, it's a big something."

"I don't know about that," Ms. Burnell replied, closely watching her daughter's reaction and trying to gauge whether she'd crossed any boundaries, "but it seems to solve a lot of your dilemma. It's like you're a surrogate for Savarna. You'd be carrying her egg. It would be her child. It would be your child. It would be your baby."

"How do I know it would even work?"

"There's no reason it shouldn't. As far as we know, you're totally capable of getting pregnant and giving birth."

Charley looked into her mother's eyes. "Her family would freak. I don't think they could..."

"They love you! Both you and Savarna have told me how much they've accepted you. You're part of their family now. I'm sure they'd understand. In fact, I'd think they would be all for it. It could be the answer to a lot of their concerns, especially about the 'lineage' thing you mentioned. It would keep their biological genes alive for another generation."

"Phew. This is big." Charley shook her head slightly. "I don't know how understanding they'd be. Hell, I don't even know what Savarna would think."

"You don't even know what YOU think about it yet."

That brought an acknowledging smile to Charley's face. "You got that right."

"It won't hurt to think about it, or will it?"

"Not literally, but… why didn't I ever think of this? Why hasn't Savarna ever mentioned it? She knows everything about this stuff. She knows every possibility."

"I'm actually a little thirsty. Could we get something to drink and look at the rest of your paintings?" Ms. Burnell rose, put out her hand and helped her dazed daughter up from the chair. As they walked back inside, she said, "Sometimes we're so close to a situation or problem that we can't see the solution, even when it's as close as our own womb? Know what I mean?"

Chapter Twenty-Six

"OK, here's the thing." Charley exclaimed dramatically. "Let me run this by you before you say anything, and I mean anything."

"Can't I—"

"Not a peep! Promise?"

Savarna nodded.

Charley and Savarna were on their porch having a late Sunday morning breakfast. The sun was shining and a warm breeze drifted under the large green umbrella above their iron outdoor table. As usual, Luscious was curled up on Savarna's lap, occasionally lifting her head to smell alluring scents that tickled her nostrils. It had been a week since Charley's mother had floated her idea by Charley, who had been stewing in its ramifications night and day.

"It's really very simple. I don't know why we didn't think about it before." Savarna started to reply, but was instantly hushed by Charley's mock gaze of admonition. "We don't have to stop trying to get pregnant. There's a very good chance we could still have your baby and adopt too." Savarna sat up, doing her best to contain her apprehension. "We could have someone else carry your fertilized egg. I could carry our baby and give birth. It would be 'our' child, 'our' baby."

Savarna sat forward, pushing the cat out of her lap, and stared in disbelief at the woman she adored. She started to speak, then looked away. She started to speak again, then leaned back in her chair and closed her eyes. The neighbor's dog barked at some noise only it could perceive. The umbrella squeaked as it slightly rotated with the hot air.

"Savarna?" Charley leaned forward. "Savarna, what do you think?"

"Do I have permission to speak now?"

"Come on. Of course."

"Where did this idea come from and why now?"

Charley moved her chair around the table and placed it next to Savarna. The legs scraped on the cement floor as she did so.

"The truth?"

"No, I only want lies."

"It was my mom."

"Your mom?"

"Well, I'd thought about it before, but she's the one who brought it up last week. Remember when I said she'd stopped by my exhibit?"

Savarna nodded.

"She said it was the perfect answer to our predicament."

"Predicament?"

"She meant, to fulfilling our desire to have a baby by birth; your parents desire for us to have a baby and everything."

"She doesn't want us to adopt?"

"Oh no! She totally is into us adopting. This is more of an adopt AND--"

"You said you've thought of this before?"

They both took a sip of coffee and tea.

"Yeah, when we first started talking about this. I've always wanted children and thought I'd be the one, but then you and your family and the lineage stuff all happened and it seemed selfish. I decided it should be you, and I've been totally happy with that decision." She placed her hand on Savarna's. "But now, now that hasn't happened, at least not yet."

"I doubt it will change. We've tried too many times at this point. For some reason my uterine lining just can't hold on to those little suckers."

"That's why my mom's idea makes sense. It can still be your egg and Johnny's sperm, but I'll carry the embryo. It will be OUR child, but yours biologically... with a little testosterone thrown in."

"Sounds like the whole surrogate route."

"Well, yes, it is, but it's me, not some stranger we put an ad in the paper for."

"My parents would freak."

"Maybe, but how could they object? Isn't this what they've wanted?

The Last Conception

We can give them the next generation, the bloodline, the whole hereditary gene thing for their faith, and have the baby we've always wanted." Charley hesitated, "Well, at least the baby I've always wanted."

Savarna turned quickly. "Hey, I know I wasn't as surefooted about all this for as long as you've been, but once I decided to go this route I've wanted it as much as you."

"I wasn't implying that you didn't. I was just remembering that I've wanted to be a mother since I was a teenager and now…" Charley leaned forward and kissed Savarna. "Now that I'm with you, the timing is right. It would have been equally perfect to have it be you, but…"

"Yeah, it's sort of ironic that as long as it didn't cross my mind it was no big deal, then when it was all I wanted it's been the only thing on my mind."

Charley caressed Savarna's forearm, as Luscious jumped back on her lap.

"I'll need to think about this," Savarna said. "You've had a head start."

"Of course."

"If we did this, we'd have to have you checked out by Dr. Matthias, and there's Johnny and my family."

"I've already made an appointment with Dr. Matthias for next month."

"I should have known."

"I'm sure it's OK with Johnny. It might not be as romantic to go to a clinic to donate instead of using our bathroom, but he'll adjust." Charley laughed. "And you know your sister and Mike will be completely supportive."

"You know it's my parents who would be the unknown factor, not anyone else." Charley nodded. Savarna finished her coffee and headed inside. "Like I said, give me a little time to catch up. Let's go for that walk at the park."

As Charley picked up the dishes and moved toward the back door, Savarna followed. "You are a real piece of work," Savarna said, as she kissed Charley, who blushed. "And I can't stop loving you for who you are."

Chapter Twenty-Seven

"Guess what?" Johnny asked.

"Don't play games, just tell me," Savarna responded as they were checking all the instruments, temperatures, freezers, and back-up systems before signing out for the evening.

"I heard that Mrs. Jamison had twins."

"That's fantastic. Boys? Girls?"

They both signed and dated their John and Joan Hancock's on the checklist.

"Two boys. Identical twins."

They gave each other high-fives as they left the laboratory and removed their gowns and gloves.

"That is such good news," Savarna exclaimed. "They tried for so long."

"You're telling me, I got really attached to them. They're a real nice family. Down to earth and realistic, know what I mean?" Johnny opened his locker and grabbed his briefcase, files, and lunch box.

"Yeah," Savarna said, as she did the same. "They are."

Johnny came up to Savarna and put his hand on her shoulder. They headed down the hallway towards the front door.

"Speaking of things working out." He cleared his throat. "Are you and Charley up for another round, or are you calling it quits?"

Savarna stopped, turned, and said, "Funny you should ask."

They stood facing each other, with Johnny's back against the white sterile-looking wall.

"I didn't think it was that funny. I was actually a little hesitant to

The Last Conception

ask. I didn't want to hurt your feelings or anything."

"I appreciate that, Johnny. The fact is, yes I have reached my limit."

"Well, that's understandable," Johnny said and started to turn away.

"But we aren't done."

Johnny stopped abruptly. "What do you mean 'you aren't done'? Reaching your limit and not stopping the whole thing don't compute."

"We've decided to have Charley carry the baby."

Johnny lowered his head, shook it side to side, then looked up and grinned. "Well I'll be. Why didn't I think of that?"

"Why didn't we think of that?" Savarna said with a bewildered smile.

"I guess we were too wrapped up in it. You know, too close."

"That's what Charley's mom implied."

"Charley's mom?"

They exited the front door, locked up, and set the alarm.

"She's the one who suggested it to Charley. It wasn't my idea at all. Caught me totally off guard."

Savarna got to her bicycle, unlocked the lock, and put on her helmet.

"Sounds like you've decided to go along for the ride."

"You bet. It's a fantastic idea. I'm just embarrassed that I didn't think of it first."

"That makes two of us. What about your parents?"

"Well, yes. There's that little problem."

"You think it will be a problem?"

"Who knows? They're always full of surprises," Savarna said as she placed her feet on the pedals. She began her ride home.

Chapter Twenty-Eight

"I know what to do," Charley exclaimed, as soon as Savarna walked in and hung her bicycle helmet on the hat rack by the front door.

"Hello. Nice to see you too," Savarna said as she went down the hall to change. Charley followed and grabbed her from behind in a bear hug and kissed the back of her neck. "That's more like it," Savarna replied. She laughed, turned around, and kissed Charley back, then went into their bedroom to the dresser and pulled out some sweat pants and took off her slacks. "So, what is it now?"

Charley sat on the bed, bouncing up and down like a child. "How to approach your parents."

"Please tell." Savarna let the elastic waistband snap around her hips, removed her sweaty white shirt and pulled a fresh blue tank top from the top drawer.

"Jordan."

"Jordan?" Savarna's eyebrows furrowed as she sat next to Charley and Luscious, who had been sneaking into the bedroom unseen, suddenly jumped up on her lap.

"Dr. Mathias."

"What about her?" The cat started purring with Savarna's affectionate petting.

"Your parents, us, Dr. Mathias, her office... don't you see?" Charley said, her head cocked sideways, a strand of her blond hair falling down her high forehead, slightly covering one bright blue eye. She brushed it aside. Savarna felt bemused and confused. Charley reached over and scratched the cat under its chin, which sent it into high drive on its purr motor. "We invite your parents to meet us at the doctor's office. We tell them we have some exciting news and want them to hear first hand. That way we can tell them what we're going to do, and the doctor can explain how it all works!"

"They'll think it's because I'm pregnant."

"Maybe that's what will get them there, right?"

"It sounds like an ambush to me."

Charley put her hands in her lap and looked out the bedroom window. "Maybe a little bit."

"A little bit? How do you think they'd feel about that, being told in front of Dr. Mathias that you, and not their daughter, was going to try to get pregnant? To top it off, we never asked for their advice about it ahead of time."

"You're right. It's a stupid idea." Charley hung her head.

"I didn't say that," Savarna replied, taking her free hand and caressing Charley's cheek. "In some ways it's brilliant."

Charley turned quickly. The bed springs squeaked. "How so? I'm confused. Should we or shouldn't we?"

"The very fact that it would be at the doctor's is a big plus. She could explain how it would work, how often it's done, and most important for Mom and Dad, that it means their bloodline could continue. Their precious teacher's lineage, tradition, and hereditary transmission would remain intact. At least in their eyes. If they don't like the idea they won't say anything in front of a stranger, let alone a doctor."

"They might be really pissed."

"Maybe, but that could be true no matter where or when they were told."

Luscious arched her back, stretched, and moved over to Charley's lap, where she was stroked and scratched. "The only thing I'm really worried about is…"

"What?"

"That it's going to be me, not you. That will be a big blow."

"It will." Savarna lay back across the bedspread. Charley lay beside her, the cat nuzzling between.

"Do you think they'll accept someone besides their daughter

carrying their grandchild?"

"Sooner or later." Savarna brushed away the hair that had fallen in front of Charley's eyes again. "They love you. You're almost like a daughter to them."

"That would be weird. Two daughters together, like us."

"You know what I mean."

"They have seemed more accepting. Ever since your mother had her heart condition and your sister adopted, they seemed to mellow a wee bit, if such a thing is possible for your mother."

"Some would say it's like Mission Impossible." Savarna giggled. "When is your appointment with Dr. Matthias?"

"About three weeks from now."

"OK. Let's put the wheels in motion when we see them this weekend."

Charley stretched over the cat, her lips slightly open, and kissed Savarna's large, beautiful nose. "I'll call and alert Jordan... Dr. Matthias... to the plan. She might have something else to suggest."

"You sure there's nothing going on with you and the doctor? You seem to be on pretty good terms."

Charley took offense. "No way. Why—"

"Just kidding." She kissed Charley on her pale cheek. "Everyone likes you. And... best of all..." Savarna paused, looking straight into Charley's sparkling eyes. "You're going to have our baby."

Chapter Twenty-Nine

Weeks passed. Savarna's parents had readily agreed to meet at the doctor's office, expecting to hear that they were going to be grandparents.

"When was the last time she, you know, attempted to get pregnant?" Mr. Sikand asked his wife as they drove to meet their daughter, her girlfriend, and their doctor.

"I don't remember." Mrs. Sikand replied. "Two, three months ago, something like that."

"I thought they could tell if someone was pregnant just a few weeks after the implant or whatever the procedure is called. If her last time was that long ago, wouldn't she have known before now?"

"I don't know," Mira said. "Hurry up. We don't want to be late."

* * * *

"Here they are," Charley said to Savarna, as Mr. and Mrs. Sikand walked into the lobby of the doctor's office. They stood as the expectant grandparents rushed over and gave them a hug.

"So, is this what I think it's about?" Mrs. Sikand asked expectantly.

"Sort of and sort of not," Savarna replied softly.

"Sort of?" her father quizzed. "What do you mean, 'sort of'?"

Savarna looked to Charley for support.

Charley took a half-step toward her possible in-laws. "It is about you having a grandchild." She put her hand on Mrs. Sikand's sleeve. "And it is about the pregnancy and carrying on your family's heritage."

"Thank goodness," Mr. Sikand exhaled. "That's what we thought.

We are so happy for you, Savarna." He gave her a hug around the shoulders.

"And for you too," Mrs. Sikand said to Charley, who blushed.

"Thanks, Mom, Dad." Savarna interrupted their congratulations. "But it's not what you think. Well, sort of, but not really."

"What on earth are you saying?" Mrs. Sikand demanded. "What is going on?" She stepped back slightly.

"Ms. Sikand," the nurse said, as she opened the door to the waiting room. Savarna and Mira both turned and said, "Yes" in unison. "Would you like to come back now? The doctor's about ready to see you."

The Sikand family, including its newest member, Charley, followed the nurse down the hall. She motioned for Charley to get up on the scale. "Let's see what your starting weight is." Charley removed her shoes and stood on the white enamel scale. The nurse moved the small weights horizontally until they were balanced at one-hundred and twenty-six pounds. "That is perfect for your height," the nurse said. She wrote down the weight on the chart and then proceeded to take Charley's temperature, blood pressure, and pulse. "Now, if you don't mind all waiting in here a few moments, the doctor will be right with you."

They entered the doctor's private office, which contained a small couch and two chairs. Mr. and Mrs. Sikand were puzzled and sat down.

"Why aren't they checking you?" Mira asked her daughter, who was sitting at her side. "Is something wrong with Charley?"

"No, she's fine, Mom. You'll see."

Davidia was leaning across his wife's lap, listening to his daughter's response to Mira's question.

"They need to make sure I'm in tiptop condition," Charley said, sitting in the chair at Savarna's side. "It's vital—"

Savarna stopped her with a slight nodding of her head. "We'll let the doctor explain."

The Sikand's were about to insist on an answer when there was a knock at the door. Doctor Matthias entered. She immediately approached Mr. and Mrs. Sikand, who stood politely.

"It's a pleasure to meet you," Dr. Matthias said, holding out her hand to the Sikands. "You must be Savarna's parents. They all shook hands. "Please have a seat," she said. She sat in the remaining soft-cushioned chair across from the family. "No doubt, you're wondering what's going on."

"Well, we assumed that we were going to hear that Savarna was pregnant, but that doesn't seem to be the case," Mr. Sikand replied.

"Is something wrong?" Mrs. Sikand asked, sitting upright, her eyes suddenly full of fear.

"No, believe me, nothing is wrong," Dr. Matthias assured her. "We wanted you to come today because there is some very good news." The elder Sikands' shoulders dropped slightly.

"The good news is," Dr. Matthias face lit up, "that you are most likely going to be grandparents, but not right away. It's still going to take some time, but there's no reason she shouldn't be able to carry a baby to term. So far, all of her tests have been normal and she appears to be quite healthy."

The Sikands both looked at their daughter, then back at the doctor. "But, we thought she was having problems, that her ability to get pregnant was questionable and nothing had worked so far."

"You are right, Mr. and Mrs. Sikand. The reality is that for whatever reason, it is very unlikely that Savarna will ever be able to get pregnant, but I'm not talking about Savarna."

"Then what the hell *are* you saying?" Davidia demanded.

"Dad!" Savarna admonished.

"That's OK," Dr. Matthias replied. "This must be confusing. The person I'm talking about is Charley, not Savarna."

Mr. and Mrs. Sikand could not hide their disappointment or surprise. They both sat back and stared at one another, than at their daughter, then at Charley, then shook their heads and glared at the doctor with the word "Why?" written all over their faces.

"I know this is different and may sound far-fetched," Dr. Matthias continued, "but it's not really that uncommon. We've done quite a few surrogate pregnancies through our office, as have other clinics and physicians all across the country."

"Surrogates?" Davidia exclaimed.

"Surrogate for what, for who?" Mira added.

"To carry your daughter's egg and give birth to your grandchild," the doctor explained. "We can implant one of Savarna's fertilized eggs in

Charley's uterus, and with a little help here and there, she will carry your daughter's child and give birth to a beautiful baby."

Davidia reached over and held Mira's hand. Their eyes met. They both shook their heads in silent disbelief.

Savarna put her hand on her mother's leg. "Mom, this will be my child... our child." She nodded towards Charley.

"It will be *your* grandchild," Charley added adamantly. "I'm just the host, the vehicle. It will still be Savarna's egg. It's coming from her, through me."

The Sikands didn't respond.

"She's correct," Dr. Matthias said. "It's very similar to what we've been aspiring to do for Savarna over the last year. We'll be removing some of her eggs, which have never had any malformations or problems in and of themselves, fertilizing them, and implanting one into a suitable host. The only difference is that it will be Charley's womb as the host, instead of Savarna's. Charley will be taking hormonal shots to prepare the lining of her uterus for the implant, just as Savarna has done, and hopefully, within the next month or two, we'll find out if Charley is pregnant and the fetus latches on to her uterine lining. If all goes well, you could be grandparents within a year's time."

"It's not the same," Mira whispered, turning to Savarna. "It's not the same, and you know it."

"Mom, it's not exactly the same, but it's as close as we're ever going to get. I thought the possibility of us having a biological child had passed, but Charley's mom suggested what we, Charley and Johnny and I, should have thought about a long time ago."

"Charley's mom?" Mira asked.

"Johnny?" Davidia wondered out loud.

"Yes, Charley's mom," Savarna said, "the lawyer in the family. She came up with the perfect solution. Dr. Matthias hadn't even said anything about it."

Dr. Matthias squirmed in her chair. "Well, no I hadn't, not yet. I was planning on doing so soon, but—"

"And Johnny," Savarna continued, looking over at her father. "You know Johnny. He's my colleague at work and also happens to be our donor. He's supported me and is more than willing to do the same for

The Last Conception

Charley."

"Supported you how? Financially?" Davidia asked.

"No, you nitwit," Mrs. Sikand replied, looking at her husband. "He's the sperm donor."

"Oh, right." Mr. Sikand blushed.

Charley leaned slightly over Savarna and addressed her parents. "It's all good, Mr. and Mrs. Sikand, and the best part, the most beautiful thing of all, is that your family and your family's ancestors' bloodline will continue. You thought it might be over, but it doesn't have to be. All these years, thousands of years, you've kept your secret and the lineage. This will make it possible to continue that tradition."

The Sikand's nodded ever so slightly, as the doctor listened without any understanding of what Charley was talking about.

"Whether it's true or not," Savarna surmised, "and you know I still think it's unlikely; but if there is any sliver of truth to the tale, then the Teacher's genes will be carried on to a new generation."

"I guess so," Mr. Sikand agreed. He and his wife squeezed one another's hands and felt some renewed hope and dawning understanding.

"Charley," Mrs. Sikand said, turning towards her daughter's partner. "I'm sorry if we hurt your feelings." Davidia nodded in agreement. "It's just been a little shock, you know?"

Charley smiled.

"You will be a wonderful mother. You're like our own family. We couldn't think of anyone besides Savarna or her sister that we love any more than you. You are giving us the ultimate gift. Thank you."

Charley went in front of Mira on her knees and hugged her lover's mother, who hugged her back. Davidia placed his hand lightly on Charley's right shoulder, as Savarna did so on her left.

"Well, I hate to break up this family love fest," Dr. Matthias said, "but if you don't have any more questions, I must be on my way. Everyone turned, wiped their eyes, and expressed their gratitude for the doctor taking the time to explain what was going on. "If anything comes up or you think of something later, and I'm sure you will, Savarna and Charley can show you how to log into our medical records and you can send me a message. I'm pretty good about getting back to you within a day or two and if it's something more complicated or confusing, I'll give you a call."

As they all stood, shook hands, and Dr. Jordan Matthias started to leave, they thought they heard her whisper, "May the fertility Goddess bless them, one and all."

Chapter Thirty

"Remember the last time we were in this office?" Savarna asked Charley, as they sat holding hands on the sofa in Dr. Matthias's office.

"Always. It's a day that I'll never forget. Your parents were amazing."

"I don't know if I'd say 'amazing,' but it went better than I'd dreamed possible."

"It's only been a few months since then, but it seems like eons ago. Shots, tests, sweet, sweet Johnny doing his part … the implantation last week… getting our final adoption application approved and meeting beautiful little Sid at the foster home. I can't believe we're already going to find out if I'm pregnant today, right now, in a few minutes."

"I know. It's sort of like a dream."

"This is what some of your clients at the fertility clinic go through."

"I had no idea it felt like this."

There was a knock at the door. Savarna and Charley gripped one another's hands tightly. Dr. Matthias walked in.

The End

About the Author

Gabriel Constans is an author, journalist, screenwriter and trauma counselor. Gabriel's fiction includes *Buddha's Wife*, *Saint Catherine's Baby*, and *Rwandan Folk Tales*. Gabriel is closely associated with *The Rwandan Orphan's Project*, *The Ihangane Project* (both in Rwanda), and *Building for Generations* (which works in Tanzania and Peru).

Website – www.gogabriel.com
Blog – www.gabrielconstans.wordpress.com
Facebook Page - https://www.facebook.com/gabriel.constans.7
LinkedIn page - http://www.linkedin.com/pub/gabriel-constans/b/b32/bb0
Twitter - https://twitter.com/GabrielConstans
Goodreads - http://www.goodreads.com/author/show/133749.Gabriel_Constans

CPSIA information can be obtained
at www.ICGtesting.com
Printed in the USA
LVHW031158250221
679923LV00003B/573